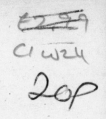
Praise for The Beggar & the Hare

'Kyrö pokes fun at the powerful and powerless, freedom and oppression, charity and greed, technology and tradition, obscurity and celebrity, Finns and non-Finns, appealing to readers with irreverence throughout. By intermingling caricature, commentary, and comedy, Kyrö concocts a cynical and hilarious world that informs one man's journey in search of a simple life of modest comfort and decent values.'

Publishers Weekly

'*The Beggar & the Hare* has a warmth, heart and humour that inspires, a firm touch on the European state of mind and European state of play, and more than enough to say about the ways of the world and its ills.'

Bookbag

'As much an exploration of Finland's relationship with its neighbours and of the nature of European capitalism as it is a witty and entertaining picaresque, *The Beggar & The Hare* is an assured and beguilingly-told modern fable.'

Booktrust

'This beautifully told fable takes a tongue-in-cheek look at capitalism in Europe today. Told with a deep affection for this loveable anti-hero, it is impossible not to fall in love with Vatanescu.'

Good Book Guide

'A delicious novel... Kyrö handles the humor and satire wonderfully, sketching a surreal vision of our modern lives.'

La Gazette Nord

'*The Beggar & the Hare* is a sweet tale of friendship and strength even during the hardest of times... Kyrö's prose is often hilarious and I found myself smiling whilst reading the closing chapters, as I felt as though I'd really travelled with our plucky hero... Similar to Jonas Jonasson's *The Hundred-Year-Old Man Who Climbed Out of the Window and Disappeared* in both style and content, fans of Jonasson's work will enjoy this slightly over-the-top tale.'

Books and Such

'Kyrö's narrative is fast and shifting: unlikely opportunities give way to unlikely accidents, and the cycle repeats itself, propelling the plot forward... *The Beggar & the Hare* is a meditation on power, politics, and celebrity. But Vatanescu's journey is also the touching story of a father willing to do anything necessary to ensure the happiness of his son; a husband who finds meaning and satisfaction in his domestic life; and a country that is slowly coming to terms with its open borders.'

The Peddle Journal

'*The Beggar & the Hare* feels fresh, funny and smart... it not only entertains, but also provides thoughtful social and political commentary on life in today's Europe.'

Maphead's Book Blog

'The best tales are always deceptively simple. They seem to be about one thing when, really, they're about another entirely. They suck you in before you know it. They have you churning and spinning, both frightened and excited at the same time. You may think you know where you are going. In truth, you don't. And neither do you, in all honesty, care. *The Beggar & the Hare* is one such novel.'

Pop Matters

THE BEGGAR & THE HARE

TUOMAS KYRÖ

Translated by David McDuff

First published in the UK in English in 2014 by
Short Books
Unit 316, ScreenWorks
22 Highbury Grove
London
N5 2ER

This paperback edition published in 2015

10 9 8 7 6 5 4 3 2 1

Original title "Kerjäläinen ja jänis"

First published in Finnish by Siltala Publishing
in 2011, Helsinki, Finland

Published by arrangement with Werner Söderström Ltd. (WSOY)

Copyright © Tuomas Kyrö 2011

English language translation copyright © David McDuff 2014

A CIP catalogue record for this book is available from
the British Library.

ISBN 978-1-78072-231-3

Printed and bound in Great Britain by
CPI Group (UK) Ltd, Croydon, CR0 4YY

The Beggar & the Hare (*Kerjäläinen ja jänis*) is a modern retelling of the Finnish classic *The Year of the Hare* (*Jäniksen vuosi*) by Arto Paasilinna.

Tuomas Kyrö (b. 1974) is one of the most versatile, prolific and acclaimed Finnish authors of his generation. His talents were first showcased in his debut novel, *Leather Jacket*, and he rose to prominence in his home country with his novel *Union*.

Kyrö draws on a long tradition of Finnish prose to tell compelling stories with great authority. He is known for the precision of his writing, exploring great passions in a laconic style. But there's another side to him – he can be mischievously witty.

Kyrö's novels have been published in French, German, Swedish, Estonian and Hungarian. He is also a prolific cartoonist and columnist.

Chapter One

In which we learn how Vatanescu goes off to be a migrant worker, says goodbye to his sister and enjoys a barbecue

There would certainly have been other alternatives; our hero could have stolen cars, salvaged the copper from telephone cables or sold his kidneys. But of all the bad offers, the one from Yegor Kugar was the best. It guaranteed him a year's employment, transport to the scene of operations and even a job for his sister, with new teeth and breast implants as a bonus.

Vatanescu left a note for his ex-wife, promising to send her child support when he had built up some income. After the divorce, his relations with the mother of his son Miklos had grown somewhat envenomed – to the point where the pus came, though both he and his ex-wife were people of good will. But when love departs, the empty place is filled by many new arrivals: envy, bitterness, revenge, shrillness, arseholery.

Vatanescu sat down on the edge of the bed where Miklos was sleeping in his grandmother's folded arms. Vatanescu removed the sock from his son's right foot and with a crayon traced the outline of the sole on a piece of paper.

You'll get your football boots.

Dad is going to fix you up with football boots.

The rust-flecked VW Transporter left the South for the North. On the hills the gearbox groaned, on the dales the brakes threw sparks, and the passengers in the rear seats were tossed about. The 'terrorist van' was of the same generation as Vatanescu, the same generation as Total Football in the Netherlands, and to be exact the vehicle had been made in the same year that Vatanescu had seen the first gleam of freedom. For although each night the only television channel in his native land had showed the same speech by the same dictator, on one occasion the pompous spectacle was suddenly interrupted by a brief flash of Monty Python. What was happening, where had it come from, the hilarious joke about the Ministry of Silly Walks?

There had been a nipple in Vatanescu's mouth that night. Mama Vatanescu had stared at the television, and along with her milk a drop of the free world, free from reason, had flowed into her son.

Vatanescu held his sister's hand as she slept in the back of the van.

If I could, I would protect you.

First I must provide for myself.

You have always protected me.

Klara Vatanescu had taken after her grandmother Murda. Brusque and efficient, in other circumstances she might have been a sturdy nomad or a foreign minister, but in the unique reality that was hers she was now joining the poorest of the poor, a woman who would have to rely on her only marketable goods. Unable to sleep, Vatanescu peered out of the rear window at the foreign church towers and remote villages inhabited by unknown people with their Teflon saucepans and digibox recorders, people who had special times earmarked for meals, for school, for sex, who had plans for the future, mortgages, visits to the orthodontist for their children, pensions, burial plots, obituaries, flowers on their graves, the whole package.

Vatanescu opened a tin. The transportation contract he had signed with Yegor Kugar included full board, which meant hammocks and corned beef. The year on the tins was 1974, and the country of origin stamped on their undersides was SWE. They had originally been intended for survival in the aftermath of a nuclear war, but to their purchaser's dismay that war had never arrived. In the nuclear-weapons-free North they grew old, so the Swedish army sold them back to the supplier it had bought them from. Who then sold them on to an international crime syndicate that used them to feed its hired workforce. The corned beef slid down Vatanescu's oesophagus, fermenting in his stomach for a while. It caused cramps that were followed by flatulence.

When Klara stepped out of the van at sunrise the following morning aeroplanes were taking off and landing somewhere far in the distance. Through the vehicle's thin walls Vatanescu could hear the engine of a luxury car idling, and he crept over to the window. Pudas, one of his fellow travellers, was complaining about the smell that floated in the van, so thick you could cut it with the tin-opener they used for the corned beef.

You can't stand the smell of a fart?

My sister is being taken from me.

They were on a stretch of derelict land. Beside the car stood some young men who, if one were to be perfectly frank, could only be called morons. Dark glasses, shell-suits of the kind worn by 1990s lager louts, their hair plastered with too much gel. The morons were trying to look like movie gangsters – in vain, for their true nature, their identity and their problems crossed all state borders. Petty dope smugglers from Poland, finger-breakers dismissed from the ranks of the Ukrainian army, playground bullies from Turkmenistan. Bullied Albanians, whom life had broken down into bastards.

Vatanescu saw one of the morons opening the door of the Mercedes. Klara leaned over to get into the back seat, and Vatanescu remembered the day he had learned to swim.

I can't swim, don't let go of me. I'm scared of water! Except... I can do it. I can swim!!!

Vatanescu pressed the tips of his fingers against the window, and the Mercedes drove off. Yegor Kugar got back into the driver's cabin of the van. He rummaged in some cassette tapes, and a moment later the music of Scorpions was heard.

Do the memories of the good times stay good even in the bad times?

It was as if the Transporter crossed a sky of lowering clouds above a churning ocean where ships laden with containers full of goods and merchandise passed to and fro. As if through binoculars you could see the sailors from the Philippines, from Vestersund and Kotka, earning tomorrow's bread, that is, the interest on their mortgages, a large bottle of Absolut vodka, their alimony payments, or the extra grand that made it possible to take their families to Thailand. In the old days only perverts went to the beaches of Thailand – nowadays it was families.

The van's rear doors opened, and Pudas and Tadas were ordered out. Their place of employment awaited them in the metro tunnel of a Stockholm suburb, where an advance guard of Finnish migrants from the pre-bag-in-box era was already at work.

Now only Vatanescu and Yegor Kugar remained in the van. The silent pair sat in the driver's cabin; the satnav gave them advice on which lanes and turnings to choose at the intersections. Their destination was the sea terminal, where Yegor steered the vehicle onto the car deck of the ferry to Helsinki.

They stepped into the corridors of a world named VIKING LINE and descended in a crowded lift to the cheapest berths.

The berths in the cabin faced one another, and when Vatanescu opened the curtains a little way he saw that there was no porthole behind them. As they settled in there was none of that horny expectancy that every schoolchild remembers from ferry crossings. Perhaps they would also be spared the exhaustion that follows adventure, and the depressing knowledge that one's virginity remained intact.

Yegor Kugar lit a cigarette by the No Smoking sign, removed his shoes and stretched his ankles for a moment like a normal human being, like a fellow passenger who in spite of being a complete stranger, a malevolent-looking one to boot, also had his good points. Vatanescu climbed up to his own berth and tested the mattress under his buttocks.

Clean sheets.

A duvet.

The ferry moved away from the quayside with a grinding sound. There came the deep note of the engines and the beercan-fuelled laughter of the teenage youths and girls in the next cabin, raucous and ringing. Yegor Kugar changed out of his designer tracksuit into a designer suit and checked his appearance in the mirror, but the expression of a highly dangerous idiot stuck there and remained.

Yegor announced that he was going to a business

meeting on the upper deck, and reminded Vatanescu of the small print in his transportation and employment contract: if Vatanescu left the cabin, Vatanescu would die. Yegor would kill him, Yegor said, exposing the handgun that was concealed under his armpit.

Do I look as if I need to be threatened?

I can't even afford a cup of coffee.

Can I afford to disobey a Russian who has only one ear?

Vatanescu had always been in trouble with the authorities. At school his teachers had seen in his flashing eyes the look of a rascal. In time the flashing had faded or been forcibly extinguished. The boy had become a man, and it is rare for a man's eyes to flash at the age of thirty-five. Little Vata's father had brandished a whip when his son misbehaved, or rather when the boy asserted his true nature, which was that of someone who likes to take things apart and put them together again. But he could not bring himself to strike his son. Instead he threw the whip into the campfire and presented Vata with a mug of steaming coffee and some bacon rind grilled on the end of a stick, a wonderful delicacy that is no longer appreciated in the Nordic countries, as one must never be able to see that the food one puts in one's mouth was once alive.

The boy's mother pulled his hair, she boxed his ears, though she loved him dearly and knew that his flashing eyes expressed his desire for life.

As soon as the bell of Yegor's lift rang, Vatanescu stepped out to the corridor. A moment later he sat in a revolving armchair on the sixth deck. The clink of bottles in the duty-free store, the electronic beeps and cascades of coins from the game machines, the hissing and whistling, the squealing and bawling of children. Vatanescu failed to perceive the division aboard the ship, a division that was as clear as a bottle of vodka taken out of a freezer. Two sorts of people shuffled or pranced across the wall-to-wall carpeting: there was the solemn group with short legs and flat noses, where the children looked like their parents. They were called Finns. Then there was the cheerful group with long legs and pointed noses, where the parents looked like their children. They were called Swedes.

Vatanescu revolved in the chair. Past him walked emaciated women and their fifteen-stone children who got out of breath on the stairs, drank lemonade and pestered their parents with constant demands. Vatanescu kicked the floor lightly with the ball of his foot, the chair spun round another forty-five degrees. Restaurants, discotheques, then the duty-free store. Vatanescu got up to look at the sea. It was getting dark. The waves had white edgings, there were lights on the archipelago. And here he was, inside this ship that was a combination of shopping centre and suburban housing estate.

Vatanescu slipped past the headwaiter who stood at a table studying the lists, and helped himself to a plateful of what everyone else was having. Salads in mayonnaise dressing, salmon in all its forms, roast meat, cold ham and cheese, sausages.

He sat down in the first vacant seat, facing an elderly couple, Pentti and Ulla or Holger and Agneta; why group them into this tribe or that, for more than their names, it was their gaze that mattered. They picked at peas with their forks and smiled sweetly, conscious of the meaning of their lives and of their approaching deaths. They existed only for each other: when one departed, the other packed bags and followed. There, today, they were the sum of their journey and their past, the sum of all the days they had been together since the spring of 1938. Their happiness, which they had paid for with their lives, was symbolised by their prawns, their slices of roast meat and their small glasses of wine.

If Miklos were here he would take the sausages first. He would remember how many he ate for years to come.

Ketchup and more ketchup. He would thank me with his eyes and I would promise that we had plenty of time to pass through the children's play area, the race car simulator and the duty-free store on our way back to the cabin.

After the Swedish nuclear-war survival rations Vatanescu's stomach was unable to cope with the super-abundance of pan-Nordic fare. A few minutes later the too-quickly reconstituted protein reserves of his body and mind would be discharged in a flood of diarrhoea. He nodded politely to Pentti and Ulla or Holger and Agneta, and then made a dash for the cabin.

If Yegor Kugar had taken a breath test he would have been well over the legal limit. So he asked Vatanescu if he was able to drive. The latter nodded, aware that the less one says the less likely one is to say the wrong thing.

Vatanescu slowly eased the van out of the mouth of the ferry into the shimmering brightness outside, from which he felt excluded. Following Yegor Kugar's instructions, he chose the green line, nothing dutiable, nothing to declare, just things to conceal, and great difficulty in changing from second to third gear. Yegor Kugar tapped the destination into the satnav, which said it was just under a mile away.

Driving behind them out of the bowels of the ship were Pentti and Ulla or Holger and Agneta. In a Nissan Primera that was always punctually serviced, and whose driver, front-seat passenger and even the car itself knew where they were going. If Pentti were to have a heart attack and die, the car would take the dead man to the driveway of his home, an oil-heated house in a rural location where each piece of furniture had occupied the same place since the Helsinki Olympics of 1952. The only object that changed position was the women's magazine that each week got moved from the television table to a bundle of old newspapers tied together with string and donated to the local junior football team's recycled paper collection.

Vatanescu drove along streets he didn't know with a man he didn't know. The sun struggled through the dirty windscreen, it was hard to make out the traffic lights, and as he focused on them he forgot to focus on anything else.

Suddenly a hare bounded out into the middle of the road.

'Go faster, run it over, kill it!' Yegor shouted.

Vatanescu turned the steering wheel the other way, the hare disappeared, and all that remained was Yegor Kugar's indissoluble rage at the fact that someone had defied his orders.

You don't run life over, you go round it.

On the corner of a street between the Art Museum and the 'Sausage' building, Yegor ejected Vatanescu from the van and threw a sheet of cardboard and an empty disposable coffee cup after him. Then he gave him a quick rundown on the terms of his future employment.

There was no question of sick leave, and he could forget about paid holidays and earnings-related social security. Yegor believed in doing things the American way. From now on Vatanescu would be on his own. Eyes down during working hours. The attitude and expression of a whipped dog. If a beggar had a smile on his face it robbed him of credibility and showed up as reduced cash flow. If you made people feel pity and guilt, one got mercy. Mercy was money, mercy was the biggest thing in Protestant religion and life in social democracies. In the Nordic countries people had such a low pity threshold that their coins burned a hole in their pockets.

'We help to make it easier for them,' Yegor explained. 'The donor ends up with a good conscience. I take seventy-five per cent, you get twenty-five.'

On the sheet of cardboard there was a description of the beggar's wretched living conditions, his impoverished poor children, his deep religious faith and his aspirations, which were rather modest. Yegor explained that one needed stories; stories breathed life into goods that would otherwise be lifeless and lacking in history. Stories brought the product closer to client, buyer and donor.

'Keep your smile up your ass, not on your face.'

Vatanescu began to feel pain instantly; he found it hard to keep his back straight. Time slowed down; the minutes were hours and the hours were the length of a whole generation. Now and then a coin fell into his disposable cup. Vatanescu would have liked to smile and say thanks, but the trick was to remain poker-faced, sad and fearful. It was best if you were able to look ugly but in a touching way.

When the daylight failed and evening arrived, Vatanescu nodded, then dozed, then lapsed into a state between sleeping and waking, and finally sank into a snoring REM slumber. There he saw pictures of things whose origin he could not account for. Firewood being chopped, logs floated, bridges under construction, a busload of people on their way to a mass suicide. Determined men of a northern land for whom everything was possible as long as they showed themselves to be persevering, creative and unyielding. The strange dream came to an end when Yegor announced with a snarl that Vatanescu had just spent his lunch break asleep.

On his first official day of work as a Romanian beggar, Vatanescu had earned five euros and eighty cents, a toy car and four cigarette stubs. Added bonuses were cold, hunger and ankylosis. He folded up his cardboard sign, put the money in one of his pockets and the begging cup in the other. In his inside pocket were the work roster Yegor had given him, a map and a tram timetable.

The metro map was just a straight line, so he managed to find the company housing before midnight. A windswept field, Caravan Number 3. Inside the caravan, somewhere in the middle of a somnolent fug, a cigarette glowed on and off. Vatanescu put his bag on a vacant bunk together with the last tins of corned beef. The smoker introduced himself as Balthazar, but Vatanescu was already asleep.

Vatanescu shook the last drops of morning urine on the gravel and prodded his memory in an effort to understand where he was and why. Which of the recent events were part of a dream, and which of them were to become reality. Around him he saw caravans, dubious electric connections, a shack and a spherical barbecue grill. In a brazier burned a fire on which a coffeepot was heating; on the horizon the city was dimly visible. Balthazar, too, now appeared in his true dimensions, and not as a mental image formed on the basis of a disembodied voice. The old man lacked an arm and a leg.

Balthazar replied to the question Vatanescu had not asked. He said he had left his arm and leg somewhere along the way, just as people always leave something behind: some forget their watch, some their heart, others leave their coat in the cloakroom. Then he thrust a bundle of newspapers into Vatanescu's hands and explained to him the importance of layers. You had to cram as many newspapers and bits of cardboard under your clothes as you could, until you could hardly move. The toilets in hamburger joints were good places for getting warm, but Yegor's men reported any unauthorised absences to their boss. There was one toilet break a day, and if you broke that rule you would have to wear nappies. If you had the money you could buy wool, quilting and down, but if the donors could see them under your rags they would feel cheated. A beggar could afford no anachronisms or breaches of style, and below a female beggar's ragged skirt there must be no flash of Manolo Blahniks, or even of fancy trainers.

Vatanescu sat in the metro, stood on the escalator, sat at his place of work. Today and from now on it would rain; autumn was here, which out in the country meant clear bright air, red and yellow colours everywhere, and rubbish burning in gardens. In the city, however, autumn was a colder, wetter and greyer affair. Vatanescu tried to empty his mind, but some advertising image or passer-by or sound always brought him back to reality.

If one forgets about the knee pain, the need to urinate, the homesickness and the shame, this is the most boring job in the world. A conveyor belt job in which neither the conveyor belt nor the worker moves, but the world does instead. How many building workers enjoy their work? How many briefcase-carrying men and suit-wearing women?

They do their share in order to obtain their share.

Don't worry, Miklos, you'll get your football boots.

When a coin fell into the cup you had to express your gratitude by an imperceptible movement of the head. Not a word, especially not in English, Yegor had instructed. You had to keep playing your part, which was that of a person who came from nowhere, understood nothing and was capable of nothing. You had to stay at arm's length, the length of two cultures. Beggar and donor had to be strangers. Any familiarity would end in acceptance, mutual understanding and a solution. Bad for business.

Passers-by who all looked the same, coming and going, never stopping. A child pointed at Vatanescu, asked his parents, 'What's that?' and received a tug at his sleeve in reply. A middle-aged man spat at him. An old woman blessed him and handed him a religious newspaper.

The average daily wage was one and a half euros, of which one euro belonged to Miklos. Vatanescu was tormented by hunger. In the stores downtown you were lucky if fifty cents bought you two sticks of liquorice. A hungry person was cold all the time, a cold and hungry person caught flu. And a person who was hungry, cold and suffering from flu did not perform well at work. The darkness repeated itself, one's head became filled with gloomy thoughts.

Why would anyone ever have wanted to live in a climate like this?

The wind is torture. The sleet penetrates one's skin.

Vatanescu had calculated that the nuclear-war survival rations were enough to last a month, but one day

Balthazar finished them off. He excused himself by saying he could not control his hand and mouth, otherwise he would never have swallowed such crap.

Hunger, the beginning and end of everything. Vatanescu sat in the buzzing metro and stared at a child several seats away, especially at the hamburger the child was munching.

Just as Vatanescu was about to lunge in the direction of the French fries, the train stopped at a station above ground where he noticed a large open-topped container in the back yard of a building.

He got out and headed for the container. People were climbing up into it. A moment later they jumped down again with full plastic bags in their hands. Vatanescu also swung himself over. The container was like something out of a children's movie, a world made of chocolate discovered in some gloomy forest. There were steaks, sausages, cartons of fruit juice and milk, cold cuts of ham and cheese, loaves of bread, oat-flakes. There were spices, strange pies filled with rice pudding; there were candy bars and condoms. Someone was throwing it all away because its sell-by date was the same as the one on the calendar.

Vatanescu did some hunting and gathering, and that evening he barbecued a kilo and a half of corn-fed pork shoulder on the spherical grill. With Balthazar, he chopped the peppers and the meat, added cream, and spiced the whole dish as only the inheritors of a rich gastronomic tradition know how. They ate it all in silence, scraped the grease and gravy from their paper plates with crusts of white bread and smiled. Everything seemed better with some food in one's belly. Next batch onto the grill, and party up!

The drinks for the pig-feast came from a cruise ship. For old Balthazar knew that the passengers on ferries from Estonia were particularly careless, and so, behind a pillar in the sea terminal, he had got his hands on three boxes of red and white nectar.

Intoxication sharpens the senses and slows the passage of time, so Balthazar and Vatanescu quietly filled their begging cups over and over again, engaging first in small talk and gradually moving on to more serious matters. Balthazar talked about the neo-Nazis in Hungary who had used baseball bats, and he talked about an old Danish passer-by who had put enough money in his cup to support him for a year, with neither demand nor explanation. He talked about his family, whom he had not seen for so long that he did not know if they were still alive, or if his wife had found another man to change the light bulbs.

The fire crackled, and the wine warmed Vatanescu's stomach and mood. Balthazar muttered that of all the people in the world the one he missed most was his mother, that ugly old witch with whom he had never stopped quarrelling.

Every day my son learns something I ought to be there to see.

Every day my son fails to learn something because I'm not there to teach him.

'Don't make life into a romantic problem,' Balthazar said. 'There's no shortage of things to complain about in everyday life. Even the owners of three-storey mansions have grievances. So do prime ministers, consultants and charismatic leaders.'

Then he opened a pack of meatballs. After that there

were grilled steaks with peppers and spicy butter.

Balthazar was afraid that his career as a wandering beggar would never take him home again. He had embarked on his foreign mission in the early 1990s, as soon as the borders were open, or rather as soon as the shrinking employment and social security options at home had forced him to cross them. He had always thought, I'll spend the autumn, winter and spring up here, and then I'll go home. But now was not the time to fret about it; today was harvest day.

Someone produced an accordion, and Balthazar played 'Mad Solsky's Polka'. He played the end of 'Summer of Tears'. He played and played, until Vatanescu lost his memory and Balthazar his sense of balance and they lay in the gravel with their arms around each other's necks, surrounded by a wasteland that had been turned into a diabolical mess.

Chapter Two

In which we learn how Yegor Kugar, a lone drug and human trafficker, grew up and lost an ear

Yegor Kugar was a professional in the security sector whose career began in the Union of Soviet Socialist Republics. Later on, the artificial Union filed for bankruptcy, but that change of affairs had no effect on Yegor Kugar's life and deeds – at least not of a negative kind. Regimes may fall, but the security police remain. The security police are the regime. From Kugar's professional point of view the nosedive of the Bolshies was actually a positive event, one that improved the state of the markets. Unstable domestic politics and power vacuums always mean brilliant new opportunities for those with no shortage of nerve and testosterone.

'I brought the poppy flowers of the mullahs to the nouveau-riche of my own land. A briefcase full of opium, several briefcases full of banknotes. Our kind of agricultural subsidy. That way the level of my income rather swiftly reached that of my clients. I bought a Nokia mobile phone the size of a beer-crate but couldn't use it to call anyone, as there weren't any network towers in our neck of the woods yet.'

At first Yegor sold sackfuls of poppies, then opium, but having been brought up on the street he soon realised that the longer a small businessman works up his raw stock the fatter his wallet will be. With his takings Yegor Kugar bought what every newly rich motherfucker throughout the world buys: an outsize four-by-four. It might do the tramcar-riding intelligentsia good to find out what it feels like to go rolling along in one's very own bulletproof, family-car-eating Hummer.

Yegor needed a temporary residence for holidays, so he bought a floor of the former Party members' apartment block. When the heroes of the Great Patriotic War on the floor above complained about the noise, Yegor bought that floor as well and moved the heroes out to the street. In his new home Yegor Kugar celebrated his own ego, the good sides of his small part in world history, among presidents, sports stars and the bearded, pointy-hat-wearing radicals of the Orthodox Church. It was an endless shindig, like the one in Yegor's favourite book *The Dirt*, which describes the everyday life – or rave-up – of the band Mötley Crüe. For in Yegor's eyes two beings were superior to all others: Vince Neil and Joe Stalin. Yegor himself puts it like this:

'I'll tell you straight, as it's important if you want to understand my character and don't just want to stick me in the slammer. I'm mad about screwing. It's the only way I know to get the shit out of my head when I'm under this goddamn stress all the time. Screwing is better than fighting, no? At first I never did drugs myself because I knew it would immediately screw up the stock records and the sales chain follow-up.

'What's the alternative? Drinking puts you out of action for several days. It's better to empty your head with screwing.

'Two weeks of business, two weeks in my pad with Miss Uzbekistan. There are all kinds of broads in the world, of all races, sizes, smells and tastes. There are the Pam Andersons and the Finnish beauty queens (but there are also the junkies, the halfwits and the Alla Pugachevas). There are the semi-uglies who are also hot nymphos in an easy-going sort of way. There are the seventeen-year-olds who look like women of thirty and there are the forty-seven-year-olds who've kept their resale value. There are the rump roasts who are bigger and lovelier than the sum of their holes. And there are the ones who are just holes, for whom I just meant money, drugs and connections; in other words a hole through which they could sniff coke with NHL hockey players. But fun was always had on both sides, until it got embarrassing, at which point I'd tell the ladies to go, and order new ones. It didn't seem possible that such a life would ever end.

'I just can't sleep alone; I need someone beside me; it doesn't matter who it is as long as she has a good body. That's how it is with the women back home, but over here the ladies have been let into the labour market; they have too many opportunities so they can let their figures go and quit wearing makeup.'

Yegor Kugar wanted more serious challenges in his life, and so he expanded his business activities from drugs to arms. A market was offered to him on a plate: hostile armies. The most important thing was that conflicts were ongoing, that no peace negotiations were started, that the situation did not become normalised. As long as the hostile army was within binocular range and antagonistic, one could trade drugs for arms.

'Shitistan, Blackanistan and blah-blah-blah. I got my supply of happy dust from the tribal warlords, paid in cash, or rather in Kalashnikovs. Then, just for form's sake, a little skirmish with those same warlords, and at the same time an application to HQ for leave, which was granted, of course, as I slipped in some powder as a sweetener.

'The problems began when the enemy side began to tighten up their morale. Worst of all were the separatists, read B-league fundamentalists, read clerics. They're an obstacle to free trade, a bit like your social democracy here. They scared the pants off me, because they weren't scared of us at all. Kind of like the Finns during the Winter War: let the Russkies bring their millions of tanks, we'll mow them down with our bows and catapults. In place of fear and flight they had hate and faith. Extremely dangerous. I respected them and despised them. But dang and drat it, if they'd gained such unlimited power, why on earth did they go on living in caves and ruins? They made threatening videos, took hostages and muttered their holy scripture, though they'd have done better to make music videos and build swimming pools in their basements with pole dancing, billiard tables and drinks cupboards.

'I realised that they didn't know much about screwing, either. That they could only get it up when they were able to rape someone. Their male cousins.'

But before Yegor Kugar occupied a position of command in the security services, before he was a drug dealer and arms trafficker, he was a zip-suited Soviet child. Mama Kugar made copious use of what analgesics and psychotropic medicines were obtainable in the army sector, and exploited to the full the limited competition that was characteristic of real socialism. It would not be unfair to call her a rather lazy and ineffectual mother.

Mama Kugar shirked as many of the aims of the five-year plan as she could, consumed her vodka by the gram and left her child to the regime. All Yegor Kugar had seen of his father was a single photo, and that photo was still in his wallet along with those of Vince Neil and Joseph Stalin. In it his father had the look of his son, the eyes of a gambler and the shirt of a sailor. A look of the kind that awakens a woman's desire but also signifies conjugal violence.

Yegor Kugar spent the first three years of his life, so important from the point of view of psychological development, on a nuclear submarine base. For eleven months of the year his father was away on assignment, and his mother was down and out at the same time. Like her only son, Mama Kugar was mad about screwing and incapable of sleeping alone, because if she did, reality and responsibility came calling. When it became clear to Yegor's father what Mama did in her free time, it took only four minutes for Yegor and Mama to find themselves standing on the potholed highway some tsar had built with serf labour for his journey to the Arctic Sea.

The father disowned his son.

Later the son disowned his father.

Such was the dough from which Yegor Kugar was baked.

School did not interest him. He began the cycle that moves from lockup to prison to reformatory to juvenile detention centre to prison camp. He was interrogated by the security police who decided that, both out of economic considerations and in the interests of reducing the homicide figures, it would be better to make the troublemaker a part of the organisation, rather than its enemy.

Training.

Hot meals.

A mattress and a blanket.

Acceptance by the community.

Yegor Kugar was not afraid of anything – he knew how to use a firearm and had no scruples about inflicting harm on his fellow human beings as long as it was preceded by an unambiguous order from above. In his gala uniform on graduation day Yegor Kugar got an erection that took control of his whole body.

The social crisis. The drug trade. The arms trade. Women.

'For a long time I stayed clean, but sure enough in the end I succumbed. I could no longer look at a Coke Zero in my hand while others were snorting happy dust, and so I discovered how to enjoy life. For me the most important thing was that with cocaine I could screw for longer.

'The gay lads from a TV interior design show came to do up my pad. That meant that more and more girls knew my door code, and the last party went on for a month. I invited Mötley Crüe to come and play and they probably did, but I can't remember anything about it.

'It's just a shame that one morning I woke up next to quite the wrong girl – a broad named Irma Mölsä with big boobs and diamond earrings who was the girlfriend of my boss, Vyacheslav Mölsä. She was a dead fish in bed, in spite of her perfect ass.

'The situation worked out exactly as we'd been taught in training school. I ended up in an industrial area of St Petersburg under the ramp in a car repair shop where a disturbed mechanic gave me a clout on the ear that seriously damaged my skull. After that I had a total blackout, but I woke up in a hospital that reeked of potatoes, missing an ear and an eye. I was alive because I was to be an example to others. That kind of thing has been going on since the time of the Romans.'

And so Yegor Kugar ended up at the hospital exit, concussed, homeless, broke and dismissed from the security police. Next he found himself sitting in the back seat of the car of a Romanian hi-fi salesman who took his rings, phone and watch as payment. The journey ended in a suburb of Bucharest, where Yegor Kugar's new career began.

'A rough country, with rough people. Damn gypsies, the lot of them. I went to night school, which means that I began to roam the streets to show them how barmy I was. That's how I began to get work. The main commodity was broads aged seventeen to thirty-four, and the main market was Central Europe. In between there were these deadly boring trips to the North to collect the pennies scraped together by beggars like that loser Vatanescu. I should never have gone anywhere near him.'

With this background it was very hard for Yegor Kugar to turn a blind eye to Vatanescu and Balthazar's barbecue feast. A beggar must not look better off than the people he is begging from; a beggar must not eat fillet steak flambéed in brandy. A fat beggar was an absurdity. Bad for business. But an even worse mistake was to oversleep in the morning.

Yegor thought that his men sprawled in their caravans or outside in the caravan park looked like pigs on some decadent farm. He said he knew that Vatanescu was behind it all; he sensed the aura of a rebel, had been able to detect such auras back when he was in the security police, possessed one himself. It usually took a man to problems, riches or a zinc coffin.

Yegor Kugar emptied the embers of the barbecue over Vatanescu. Yegor Kugar locked the doors of the caravans. Yegor Kugar said there would now be a week without pay and a twenty-four-hour workday. Go away and shake off those calories, and don't come back until you look like what you are, not like homeowners in some plush suburb!

Chapter Three

*In which we learn how Vatanescu burns his bridges and
meets his soul-mate*

Yegor outsourced the most unpleasant tasks to the
Svetogorsk Speedfreaks. The Speedfreaks cut off
the electricity to the beggars' encampment at 7pm and
made sure there was no surplus food or pleasure in the
caravans. The lights came back on at five. When this
was combined with a darkness that fell ever earlier, an
increasing amount of rain, a strong wind that brought
an icy chill, and the reluctance of people to part with
their small change, Vatanescu sank into dejection. The
passers-by snarled, spat – even the woman who distributed the religious newspaper hurried rudely past on her
way to holy-roller meetings held in old cinemas.

The streets are amazingly clean.

Am I the only rubbish?

Balthazar consoled him, telling him that his anger
would eventually subside, but Vatanescu saw no further
than the following day, and not even that far. He had the
same symptoms of burnout that afflicted the givers of
alms. People wanted to get back to their communally
heated homes by the quickest possible combination of
bus, train and walking, and they did not feel obliged to
help a person who was capable of working.

Inevitably the day came when the Organisation gave
the order that there must be more results. There were
to be discussions about layoffs, because International
Crime was a supranational company listed on the stock

exchange, just like Nokia or Gazprom. Moreover, the Organisation's advertising and marketing department noted that the public image of begging had taken a battering. The police were tackling the beggars ever more snappishly, and public opinion was hardening by the day. The mayor wanted the ragged riff-raff off his streets.

The Organisation's head office demanded increased productivity. They must all increase their output by thirty per cent, and at the same time the least productive ones would be fired. Those who had arrived last would be the first to go. The row of beggars listened to Yegor's speech, Vatanescu slightly apart from the others on the steps of his caravan. His nose was running; perhaps it was fever, maybe hypothermia was setting in.

Yegor Kugar.

To you a quiet stretch of water is a place where you can duck the head of your fellow man and drown him.

And inevitably the day also came when the camp was filled with the flashing blue lights of police cars, and after them the flashing red lights of bulldozers. The police gave the residents five minutes to gather their belongings and then return to the land of their fathers. The women and children would be guaranteed a place in the warmth of a shelter for the night, and would be taken there locked up in a Black Maria.

As usual, the adult male simply had to manage. The adult male only has what he takes, and he invariably takes it from others. This produces accusations, demands for compensation and world wars. Because adult males are the cause of everything, they are sent off to the worst places, to hunt, to fight wars, to build playhouses for children, to take part in the Finlandia Ski Marathon – though they'd willingly rush to put on skis themselves. The adult male is useful as long as he is strong. As long as the adult male is able to defend and protect his family, he has a purpose as a threat to those outside his intimate circle. This show of strength produces all the good things and bad things in the economy, rock music or even the arms trade, for example. Sad is the lot of the wretched man who cannot seize what comes his way, the lot of the man who is unable to fight for his place in the sun, who does not master the language, the tricks of the gambler or the comedy that softens the fall. A man does not arouse pity as a child does, or desire as a woman does: his fundamental role, and the meaning of his whole existence, is to produce economic added value.

I am no use to anyone.
No one is any use to me.
I am not needed.
I need football boots.

The bulldozers bulldozed and bashed and lifted the debris into a skip. As Vatanescu stood with Balthazar and the other beggars in a nearby pedestrian underpass, the old man took his hand and pressed it as a father would press the hand of his son, transferring all his strength from himself to his successor. A firm pressure, cold, wrinkled palms. Balthazar said he had seen in the stars, or rather knew from experience, that no good ever comes of a grilled steak. Right at that moment, for the first time on his journey, Vatanescu began to feel something: first fear, then uncertainty, and then a sense of being mightily pissed off. Vatanescu jabbed his fist into the wall of the underpass – he who had never hit anyone. He pumped himself into the state that made possible the events that followed.

When the figure of Yegor Kugar appeared in the entrance to the underpass, Vatanescu knew that he for his part was not going to retreat. The bulldozers were leaving; now he must be as strong as they were, he must bulldoze his way forward, even though he had no idea where it might take him. Their homes were destroyed, their source of income removed, and what did Yegor Kugar do? He asked the brothers Vatanescu and Balthazar if now they understood the general situation.

The general situation?

Here everything is a matter of individuality.

Individuals. Private property. An independent professional's right to a pair of football boots.

'Have you got it through your thick skulls, or do I really have to explain to you why negotiated layoffs are necessary?'

For the first time, Vatanescu stared Yegor Kugar in the eye.

Pig.

Yegor heard the whisper. After a moment of silence, the kind of silence during which a man like Yegor Kugar decided if he was going to rearrange one's features with his fist there and then or if he had better resort to the socially more acceptable art of verbal humiliation, he said quite calmly that Vatanescu was dismissed from his duties. Vatanescu's eyes narrowed. Yegor Kugar relates:

'I sent him on his way. Fired him for breach of trust. Deleted him from my email address book. One man whom begging doesn't need. This is not a benevolent fund; it's subject to the same laws of supply and demand as any other business. I sold these guys, I invested in them, so they had to bring me some returns. Vatanescu was a liability right from the start. I forbade him to work in any of the areas controlled by our Organisation – any country, city, village with more than seven thousand inhabitants or a floorball club anywhere in Europe. Because I'm a good man I gave him an early retirement plan, a pension package and protection from dismissal. I gave him twenty euros.'

A twenty-euro note in his hand. Nearby, a camp that had been wrecked. No way of making a living. Now there were no more alternatives, and Vatanescu let his body do what it wanted to do. He crumpled the money in his fist, took a step back and lashed out with his arms at Yegor Kugar. From somewhere he had found the strength he ought not to have had. He added a head-butt that made Yegor lose his balance and fall to the pavement.

Balthazar sat on top of Yegor. Then, one by one, all the other beggars did the same.

Vatanescu snatched the wad of banknotes from Yegor's hand and ran as he had never run before.

One day something happened to Vatanescu's home village. It was demolished. Farewell to the mill and the centuries-old stables with their stone foundations. The site was levelled and fenced off, and a mobile phone factory built on it. Vatanescu had once applied to work there, but a monkey would have had more luck in getting a job than Vatanescu, for at least a monkey has job options in zoos and on cartoons. Only the cottage belonging to Komar Tudos had survived. It survived as it had done throughout all the upheavals in Europe since the days of Byzantium. Perhaps so that later it would be discovered by some opinionated documentary filmmaker from the North who would obtain a grant and prizes for Komar Tudos on the strength of his story. Or perhaps because the world changed, but Komar Tudos never did. Each morning Komar stepped into his back yard, spat once to the left and three times to the right, greeted all the ghostly beings that whirled around him and visited his outside toilet. The cart track that passed in front of the Tudos cottage had been traversed by Nazi armies, Communist armies and Coca-Cola trucks, and was now about to be surfaced with asphalt.

Komar smiled. Or was it the semi-paralysis of his face that twisted the old man's expression?

Vatanescu had a wad of criminal cash, four hundred and eighty euros. When one started with nothing, five hundred was almost the stuff of legends, and it would at least enable him to buy the football boots. First thing in the morning, as soon as the sports shops with their vast windows opened their doors, Vatanescu would go inside and choose the boots that were worn by the best and most expensive players of the day. And what remained would form the basis of something greater.

Without a purpose, what I've done is merely the insane action of a man who has been driven to the brink.

Just as everything that people do often is.

Give it a purpose.

Give it a meaning.

Vatanescu's joy in the money disappeared when he realised that what he had done might equally have been the most stupid act of rage in the world of bipeds, something for which he would have to pay interest at far above the market rate. When the word got around, when mobile phones connected Finland to Vatanescu's home village in Romania, information about the solo beggar would reach Yegor's henchmen.

Vatanescu sat down on a park bench between the large white building of Finlandia Hall and the inlet that comes in from the sea. On the other side of the bay a goods train rumbled. He tried to curl up in his own armpit, tried to forget the cold. In spite of the adrenaline and the cold, his constant tiredness got the upper hand. But we shall not let Vatanescu fall asleep.

The bushes rustled.

Something moved.

Vatanescu wondered if there were snakes in this land.

Then from the south he began to hear a babbling that grew into a unique and universal shouting. The shouting approached at a running pace; a group of young men threw stones and brandished sticks. Vatanescu was surprised that Yegor had managed to send a gang of assailants made up of local residents after him so quickly.

Don't kneecap me.

Don't torture me. Don't kill me.

The youngsters ran past Vatanescu towards a bush.

As the crime squad combed the bushes for something, a creature hobbled out from between their legs. Vatanescu caught it in his hands and hid it in his jacket.

Whatever you are, you are smaller than that group of human animals.

The youngsters' heads popped up from the bushes. They noticed Vatanescu and asked if he had seen a nasty rodent. A pest that was a menace to the city, gnawing the roots of the apple trees on housing estates and rushing about in the traffic causing unnecessary insurance claims. The youngsters were paid five euros per rabbit; the city's zoo bought the long-eared creatures to feed to the tigers.

Vatanescu felt the small creature's heart beating against his, and nodded.

I saw it. It went that way. Towards the railway station.

If you're quick you'll be able to catch it.

Go on, hurry up, or it will get away.

When the lynch mob had disappeared from view, Vatanescu looked at the rabbit that was furtively flattening its ears in the shelter of his jacket. The poor thing's gaze was weary, and it begged for mercy.

Don't be afraid of me, I'm Vatanescu.

Like you.

Tiger food.

Vatanescu washed the undernourished creature in seawater and noticed there was a splinter in its paw. When he pulled the splinter out the rabbit gave a piteous squeal and the wound began to bleed more profusely. In Vatanescu's family there were fortune-tellers and soothsayers, but he himself had as scientific a view of the world as a man who was self-educated could have. Yet, precisely for that reason, this rabbit that had sprung out from nowhere in front of him seemed too powerful an omen to be the result of mere chance.

I must save you. Then I will save myself, too.

I have no one here. I have no one in the world but my son Miklos. We are going to help each other, we are going to manage. Let's start with you.

With the rabbit in his pocket, Vatanescu set off for the city's main thoroughfare. A red cross on the street signs guided him to the nearest emergency clinic.

The name above the hospital entrance was that of Miklos's mother, Vatanescu's ex-wife.

Chapter Four

In which Vatanescu meets Hertta the philanthropist, Keijo the verger, Usko Rautee and Ming, and in which he becomes an international investor

The sliding doors of Maria Hospital's first-aid clinic opened at regular intervals. At the reception desk sat Hertta Mäntylä, a woman of strong personality praised for her skill in showing sympathy, someone who was able to give silent support to others in sorrow, pain and uncertainty, without being alarmed or frightened by the situation. During the night she had admitted Valdemar Kiminkinen, born 05.06.64, who had struck his head on the pavement as a result of drunkenness. It was also possible that Kiminkinen had been involved in a dispute with his partner, but the partner's name escaped him for the moment. What he did remember was a race that had been run at Turku athletics stadium in the 1960s, and a life that had gone wrong. Kiminkinen was not bitter, but he kept saying that he wanted to start from the beginning again.

Hertta helped Kiminkinen to lie down and advised him to stop drinking. She even whispered in his ear that love would be the best remedy. But the possibility of that was vanishingly small.

Ticket Number 106 belonged to Liisi Tunder, born 12.12.20, Sagittarius, an old lady who had preserved her beauty in age. Currently she sat on the other side of the glass partition of Hertta's reception desk, but her mind travelled the roads of her childhood in a hired car driven by her chauffeur Alzheimer. Mrs Tunder had been found almost naked in the street, wearing surgical stockings and holding a coffeepot. She was asking passers-by if the air raid was over, and why she could not find her best friend, Ulrika. Mrs Tunder was accompanied by a man of the same age, anxious and perplexed – her husband. Hertta had booked a room for him at a nearby hotel. A needle was inserted into Mrs Tunder's birdlike arm, she fell asleep and Hertta thought how many people there were in the world who needed to be limitlessly stroked.

The next customer approached the reception desk without a ticket, blood streaming from his nose. Flägä. Unable to remember his date of birth. Did remember taking Temgesic tablets and also injecting some as yet unnamed liquid narcotic. Had a strong sense of split personality and wanted to escape from the world of Lord of the Weasels, wanted out of Manacles of the Sixth Neuron. As Flägä could not be hugged, he was tied down with hand restraints, something that had had to be done the previous week, and would be done again and again, until he attained prison, death or Salvation.

Oh the dear children, oh the life and the longing, oh the bullied ones, Hertta thought. Oh the lack of love, the cold atmosphere at the breakfast table, the lonely journeys to school, a world where only chemistry helps, not money or a neighbour. Oh your need to forget things that will probably never happen to you. Oh why don't you leave chemistry for school lessons, why don't you quit cutting classes and get your qualifications for working life?

Vatanescu was sitting some ten yards from Hertta. He kept the rabbit hidden inside his jacket, not daring to look at anyone but the pigtailed little girl who smiled opposite him with life and joy in her maybe six-year-old eyes. The sticking plaster on her arm said that she had had a blood sample taken, and the heroic deed had been rewarded with an ice cream on a stick. Her tiny teeth nibbled at the chocolate and her tongue licked the vanilla that appeared underneath.

The rabbit tried to abandon the sleeve for freedom, but Vatanescu stopped it. The rabbit tried to leave by way of his collar, but Vatanescu put his hand in the way. The little girl spotted the rabbit and continued to lick her ice cream. Children are less surprised by unusual things than they are by ordinary, conventional ones.

The girl's mother wondered who her daughter was making faces and smiling at – was it that foreign tramp who smelled of sewers? The rabbit retreated back into the sleeve. Vatanescu looked away, and as they continued to play their game the queue numbers changed; there were still twenty to go until it was Vatanescu's turn. The girl fell asleep in her mother's arms. Vatanescu felt tired as he looked at the weary, flu-ridden people, the stooping and the stooped. Behind the Venetian blinds one could hear the city waking up to the morning; the streetlights were going out. In their place the sun tried to break through the veil of cloud, and Vatanescu sank into slumber.

He woke up when the little girl tapped his knee with her finger. She was pointing to the number on the board and the number on Vatanescu's ticket.

The dictatorship under which he had grown as a child had given Vatanescu a knowledge of languages. At school in 1984, before the Los Angeles Olympics, he had distributed official brochures sponsored by a soft-drinks company, for Romania was the only country in the socialist bloc apart from China that took part in those Games. The heroes of Vatanescu's childhood were athletes with names like Nadia, Ilie and Cojocaru.

He read the brochures in their original language, deciphering them syllable by syllable until he began to understand what he was reading.

Hertta Mäntylä saw before her an English-speaking vagabond, but that was no problem as long as he had a health insurance card. From Hertta's point of view Vatanescu looked tired, possibly depressed, and perhaps he was suffering from seasonal influenza. Years of experience told her that for most of the patients sleep was a better remedy than treatment, institutionalisation, pills and injections. Sleep, unbroken and secure, that began under clean sheets in a well-aired room. A process of waking that took place in one's own time, to the smell of coffee, with a newspaper. In a house of kindly women, uncles with a sense of humour, small children playing sweetly and quietly, full of life. If only one could give that to people, instead of always being in a hurry, busy earning one's living, with a fear of death and a constant sense of fatigue. The circles under one's eyes, the tyres under the leased car, the fire under one's arse, the flame under the spoon, here under the North Star. People needed to be taken by the hand. People needed to be taken to Linnanmäki Amusement Park, to the fells of Lapland, where they could let the wind caress their pockmarked skin and scarred souls and blocked emotions. There were so many places where they could find the life they silenced in themselves.

'Änt wot is joo problem?'

Vatanescu said something about broken bones, a bleeding hind-leg and a gang of boys who were in pursuit. Hertta looked at him – he didn't seem to have any broken bones. The one thing that Hertta could not abide was people who made unnecessary visits to the emergency clinic, wasting the taxpayers' money on imaginary complaints. The world could not take any more malingerers. She asked Vatanescu if he had a health insurance card. No, he didn't. A passport? No. An identity card? No. A social security ID? A fixed address? No.

Hertta rose from her ergonomic chair. If the trouble was serious, Vatanescu would receive treatment, but if this were some kind of fraud, it had to be exposed. Hertta told him to show her the injured limb. Vatanescu pulled the rabbit out of his sleeve.

But how could he have known that Hertta Mäntylä detested animals? She was allergic to all living beings except human ones; animals caused her to swell up, they covered her in spots and made her sneeze. In Hertta's view of the world mammals had a clearly defined place, and the South Helsinki Health Clinic was quite the wrong place for rabbits. They belonged in nature; they spread disease, put their paws on you, licked you with their revolting tongues, panted, growled, nibbled. Through her increasing panic she whispered that this was not a vet's surgery. Vatanescu tried to explain that the rabbit had very probably been born in Finland, somewhere in the area between the Botanic Gardens and the big blue hospital. So perhaps it could be given a social security number and thereby the right to medical treatment.

Hertta Mäntylä screamed as though Vatanescu had put a machete to her throat or threatened to blow up the hospital. Hertta Mäntylä pressed the panic button and announced through the loudspeaker that the police were already on their way. Hertta Mäntylä covered her face with a surgical mask, closed the window of the reception desk and refused to work any more.

Vatanescu made quietly for the exit; he must leave this place, avoid the handcuffs. The rabbit's paw hung limply. From its mouth came a pitiful whimpering. And although the use of a fluffy animal and a little girl in the same scene would be pathetically melodramatic, it really did happen that the girl ran after Vatanescu. She held out the stick that was all that remained of her ice cream, and undid the laces of her little red shoes.

You wise little person.

Opposite the hospital was a cemetery, where in the stillness Vatanescu used the stick from the little girl's ice cream to make a splint, which he fixed to the rabbit's paw with one of the shoelaces. Raking the gravel paths between the dark gravestones was an old man who raised his hat. When Vatanescu nodded, the old man mounted the steps that led to the rear door of the chapel and soon returned with a thermos flask.

The man's face was fluted by the winds of the north, and his handshake was firm.

Why do I want to cry?

Suddenly I have a sense of complete security.

When the man poured him a cup of hot coffee, a tear ran down Vatanescu's cheek. The man nodded and wiped the tear away. Vatanescu looked the man in the face.

You accept me. You let me be myself.

Thank you.

You're a human being.

The man had a ham sandwich, which he divided in three, and a cupful of milk for the rabbit. It drank eagerly. The old man gave Vatanescu a handkerchief. They had no common language, but it is easy to express gratitude without words, by taking someone's hand in one's own. They were able to exchange names: the old man's was Keijo.

The verger led Vatanescu and the rabbit into the chapel so they could warm themselves and gather their strength. They would be able to rest there until the daily work of the chapel began and the space was needed for the mourners. The organist was practising in the organ loft, a warming sun shone through the high windows. Now and then it vanished behind clouds. Vatanescu fell asleep feeling better, as the top end of the hierarchy of his basic needs had been satisfied: he had obtained food and warmth, and the rabbit had received first aid.

The prosaist Helinä Halme lived until she died. In literary circles Helinä was known as an author of highly charged autofiction, a shameless scrutiniser of private pain spots and an original interpreter of her own generation. In the real world of her children Heikki and Kaija, Helinä Halme was known as a self-centred and manic-depressive mother for whom family life meant demands and victimisation. It was true that as an author she had the right to make use of material from her own everyday life in her books, but the more that Helinä Halme revealed in her writings, and the greater the interest of the media, the greater the discomfiture of Heikki and Kaija. In her books Helinä Halme understood the world and man; she understood society and the individual; she engaged boldly in polemics, possessed a virtuoso mastery of language and could be both hard-hitting and tender. At home, however, she had no sense of proportion. Through the pain that mother and children experienced, their relationship could have grown more mutually influential, in an adult and balanced way, but the Grim Reaper had made Helinä Halme collapse onto the picture of the apple on the lid of her laptop. From her mother she had inherited a latent heart defect.

Heikki and Kaija's father did not come to the funeral. He had severed relations with his former spouse when she published her final, breakthrough work *The Fist Talks, the Man Doesn't*. 'Each punch unforgivable, even the ones that were never delivered, but which I saw in his eyes.'

Heikki had not wanted any of his mother's belongings. Kaija did not refuse the art deco furniture, the shares and the savings account. The books they donated to the second-hand bookshop on the ground floor. For the apartment they asked a price that meant it sold within a week.

At last, was Kaija's first thought on the death of her mother. Heikki had burst into tears, and after a day spent sobbing had called the undertaker's office. No big funeral, no Karelian hotpot. A simple urn. An obituary notice in the newspaper; as epitaph a line from one of Helinä's own poems from her collection *The Apple Tree Has the Colours of Chile*.

The children's Uncle Pertti attended the chapel. A childhood shared in common generally makes people cry at funerals, even though as adults they may have ploughed very different furrows. Heikki, Kaija and Uncle Pertti were seated in the second row. When the organ began to play, a man whom no one knew emerged from the front row. A tramp.

Vatanescu nodded to Helinä Halme's family and walked out of the chapel.

From the point of view of Vatanescu's story the Halme family is not important. More important is the tabloid journalist who secretly photographed the mourners from the front seat of his car. Vatanescu did not notice the journalist, and of course the journalist did not recognise Vatanescu, but the picture he took began to circulate on the Internet. Vatanescu was identified in the background of the funeral photo; someone enlarged it and realised that the same homeless individual could be seen in a video that had been taken with a mobile phone at the Maria Hospital. An ill-dressed but sympathetic looking man was glimpsed showing the duty nurse what looked like a hamster or some other pitifully wriggling creature.

The football boots.
Vatanescu found the tram stop and travelled to the city centre.

He looked for a sports shop.

He looked for the footwear section.

He looked in his pocket for the piece of paper on which he had traced the sole of his son's foot on the day of his departure.

How long is it since I left? Is there a table that would show how much the foot of a boy of that age would have grown?

Studs, laces, Velcro, glitter, stripes, oak leaf, riders, spinners, joggers, runners, there was no mode of human progression that would not have required its own footwear. Vatanescu compared the various items of footwear with the foot he had drawn on the paper.

Nike?

Adidas?

The most expensive ones would take all Yegor's money; those are the ones I need. A parent's job is to guarantee his child a better life than his own.

A girl wearing a T-shirt with the shop's logo approached Vatanescu. Vatanescu selected the most expensive boots and asked her to wrap them up. Just to make sure, he showed his banknotes.

Where is the post office? Where can I send them from? My son is going to be a striker. A goalscorer. He's going to be admired, like the car I'll take him to practices in.

The salesgirl took the boots from Vatanescu.

She made a sign to the assistant who was in charge of the dietary supplements counter, a mountain of muscle who looked like Lex Luthor and began his day by shaving his entire body, after which he drank a pitcher of protein milkshake and deposited a bloody stool in the john. Steroids will do that, but a price must be paid in order to make your veins and muscles stand out and your neck swell like a nuclear-power station about to explode on the coast of Japan. By this time Lex's penis was tiny, his testicles the size of raisins, he could no longer get an erection, but who cared when he could lift five hundred pounds of cast iron from the weights bench? Lex's real name was Rahikainen. A Lion of Finland pendant hung round his neck and he was a good and warm-hearted man, but had always hated gypsies. He had been frightened of them ever since he was a child; in the shopping mall they tried to sell you watches or drugs or steal your tram season ticket and your pocket money, threatened you with a knife, or with their brothers. He should not be seeing one of them here in the shop, because as far as he knew not many gypsies ever bought sports items for their own use.

Without a word Rahikainen walked up to Vatanescu. He lifted him by the scruff of his neck, so that the rabbit started to fall out of his armpit. Vatanescu managed to seize the rabbit by the ears and thrust it back inside his jacket. Rahikainen carried Vatanescu outside. He threw him on the pavement, under the feet of the passers-by, back to his origins.

'We choose our customers.'

The boots don't only have a price, they also have a customer's face.

How can I get a face like that?

One mustn't be wretched, one mustn't be a beggar, the lowest of the low. One mustn't be a leech sucking the excess from the well-to-do.

One must be one of them.

I don't know their language; how can I be part of the group? They don't like music, they don't like barbecues, they don't like cheerfulness and they don't like apathy.

Work.

Work is what they like. The Finns like someone who works.

One day Yegor had said to Vatanescu: 'Dole money would get us a much more predictable and easier cash flow than begging. All that you men and women of the sixth European division need is a social security ID. It's a secret passage straight into the cash tills of the job agencies, into income support, pensions, the lot, study grants, housing grants, all of it earnings-related. Stipends from the Cultural Fund and the Kordelin Foundation. When a person is just a number on a computer, that number can go on raking in money forever. Seventy-five per cent to me, twenty-five to you.'

Usko Rautee steered the spoon to his mouth, spun his revolving chair round and looked out of the morning window at his home town. It was at once beautiful and ugly, like life or Yoko Ono. Or like Usko's clients. The flavour of the yoghurt was nothing-with-the-addition-of-something-slightly-unpleasant.

Church towers and factory chimneys stood silhou-etted against the sky, between them a mass of build-ings, from the beautiful constructions of the nineteenth century through the monstrous creations of the 1970s to the insipid vanities of the 2000s. Though their original meaning had been lost, the church towers and factory smokestacks were still there. The production work of the factories had been moved to countries where costs were lower, the industrial halls converted into floor-ball courts or television studios. While people still got married in the churches, God had left the building, left the whole planet, and had moved on to the next galaxy.

Usko Rautee scraped the last spoonful from the bottom of the yoghurt carton and felt the absence of God. Yoghurt promised today's stressed individual the same benefits the Church had earlier. Eternal life, mental equilibrium, more energy for one's work and, after repentance, heaven. In order to get there one did not even have to die, merely get on with one's life.

The yoghurt had a nasty taste, but there was no such thing as a free lunch. Saints had always endured priva-tions and suffering.

Usko had grouped his clients into three main categor-ies. The first category were the coasters. The coasters, and the world, were like mercury and Teflon. The only things that stuck were the pizza crumbs on their shirt-fronts and their hands on Mum and Dad's wallet.

Usko opened another yoghurt and wondered when the world had got like this. Nowadays every kid who dropped out of suburban high school had the rights of a prince and the living standard of an earl. It was the result of progress, comfort and low prices; it was splendid and totally monstrous. It had begun with the invention of the axe, continued with the concept of the wheel, and moved on through the mass production of cars to this world where there was a gaming console in every room. Sliced bread in the kitchen. A helmet on one's head and reverse parking radar in one's car.

What can one demand of a person who is born into this world? Nothing, because one is born into it as a customer, and one cannot demand anything of a customer; customers have to be served. The coaster knows exactly the level he wants to coast towards – a celebrity, a poker star or a mogul – without having the slightest idea of how he is going to get there. The coaster wears slip-ons until he dies because he never learns to tie his shoelaces.

Usko felt sorry for them, and had a sense of being different. He felt sorry for himself, too, he who had to eat health food yoghurt so he could live his life to the end. In the 1970s, in the same kind of problem environment, one was allowed to drink vodka. But now those years had to be paid for with these yoghurts.

Cleaning work – the cleaning and hygiene sector – was a gauge of social progress, just as the prison industry once had been. Office cleaning jobs did not suit the coasters. The starting pay was too low, the status of heavy manual labour insufficient. The few coasters who did accept the jobs that were offered to them fell asleep in a corner of the printing works they were supposed to be cleaning.

But coasting is always relative to the degree of responsibility. With enough debts, children and alimony payments, even the coasters reach for the spray bottle.

The baldies were a more tragic group. Their jobs had disappeared at the same time as the electric type-writers had vanished from government offices. In their day the baldies had been machine draughtsmen and system administrators at the spearhead of progress, but six years on they were now on the scrapheap or needed only for children's games. Unlike the electric typewriters, the baldies had neither the outer casing nor the inner padding to be able to sit on the living-room floor and be hammered by a three-year-old. At some point they began to feel they could do with a beer, even if they didn't like beer. A Big Number 4, no, make that two, and a shot of vodka. Their work was now being done by computers, and there was no way out of that.

If you offered the baldies an office-cleaning job, their livers or knees were in such a fragile state that they had no hope of being able to manage the floor polisher. The baldies weren't lazy in the same way as the coasters, but they had an over-developed sense of self-esteem, which could certainly tolerate decades of hard drinking – from earnings-related income support all the way to unemployment pay – but not a promising career in the cleaning sector.

As Usko spooned down his yoghurt, he felt his thoughts quicken. The jobs didn't go to China because some arrogant capitalist took them there, but because the consumer wanted to buy cheap stuff. The customer wanted to save money. So why not let him, and sell everything cheap? Nowadays everyone had the chance or the wealth or the credit or the short-term loan to buy everything. It was there – in the cutting of prices – that democracy functioned most indisputably.

The third group that Usko encountered on a daily basis were the highly educated arts graduates, who would only take jobs in their own field. If their own field was ethnology, and their specialist subject the development of Judinsalo distaffs and their influence on the metrosexual dandies of the freehold estates in 1780s Finland, Usko was powerless to do anything about it. When he offered this highly educated group that vacant office-cleaning job, they asked if it was a classical paradox, a metaphor or a stigmatisation. The arts graduates lounged off with their shoulder bags to the vegetarian restaurant across the street to wait for a grant that would never come. Bitterness arrived instead.

Usko put the lid back on his carton of yoghurt, placed the carton on the windowsill and wiped his moustache. He cleared his throat, got up from his chair and opened the door to the hallway. Someone was sitting in the waiting room.

'Come i-i-n,' Usko Rautee said without looking up. Then he put on his glasses and roused his computer from its sleeping state.

Usko smiled at the client; that was how he always began. Each someone was an opportunity, at least for themselves. For the system, each someone was an opportunity to remove that someone from the system.

The someone was a tired and wan-looking man who had been fired from his regular job and was ready to accept any kind of work. As work experience the man listed construction, tending livestock and cutting out half-length paper silhouettes on the corner of Bucharest Park Street and Ceausescu Square. A quick learner, not given to complaining. No references or letters of recommendation, but as a sample of his work Vatanescu snatched up a pair of scissors that were lying on the desk and a blank sheet of paper from the printer, and in a few seconds cut out a very lifelike silhouette of Usko Rautee. Usko Rautee asked if Vatanescu was prepared to do something different from creative improvisation. Was he capable of real work?

You have the means to distinguish between real work and false work.

Hire my head, my hands and my feet for eight hours, determine my wage and pay me at the end of the day.

I want the football boots.

Usko Rautee typed Vatanescu's details into the computer and pressed Enter. Alternatives were offered: Vatanen, Esko; Valtaoja, Esko; Vataranta, Essi; Valamo Etruscans. Usko studied the computer screen, shook his head and muttered to Vatanescu what it said.

Vatanescu did not exist.

Create me. Please.

Rautee tried F1, F5 and Ctrl+V, but Vatanescu still lacked a social security number – in other words everything. It would have helped if Vatanescu had an ID in his own country, but that too was lacking. Usko said he would try to create Vatanescu. First he would have to fill in a questionnaire that would outline the foreign worker's qualifications in the Finnish labour market.

Did Vatanescu speak Finnish?

No.

Did he have a fixed address?

No.

Usko looked at Vatanescu's weary eyes. He wasn't a coaster or a baldie or an arts graduate. He was a man, capable of work, willing to work, and of working age. He didn't even look as though he had problems with alcohol. Yes, he smelled, but the reason for that was his unwashed state, not drink. In order to be able to work he didn't need eight years of training, just a little soap.

Usko leaned round his computer and asked Vatanescu if he was really willing to do any kind of work.

I'm in the shit. A people smuggler wants my head. I'm being hunted.

Must I rob a bank?

If the conveyor belt below the factory smokestack that was visible through the window still worked, Vatanescu could be sent to work on it, or perhaps to the packing department, or perhaps as a pusher of wheelbarrows.

He could unload containers at the harbour. Jobs like that didn't really need to be entered on the payroll, Usko reflected.

He looked Vatanescu in the eye.

'I'll take you on myself. I'll hire you.'

You'll fire me?

Usko pronounced the word more distinctly and made it clear that this was a labour contract. If you wanted a service society, you had to get on with the work.

'A service society. A customer-oriented society. That's what you hear everywhere. Vatanescu, you can be my servant. How would you like that? Another name for the job would be general dogsbody. I'll pay you a decent wage and sort out your social security for you. You'll do cleaning. Wash my car. You'll take hot meals to my mother three times a week. OK? Is it a deal?'

Vatanescu did not manage to say anything, as the rabbit was struggling inside his jacket.

Usko Rautee said he would make the offer as honest as was possible in these doubtful times. Vatanescu would have the weekends to himself, and they would agree on when he could take his autumn, winter and summer holidays. Usko Rautee felt that for once he was doing something, not just following the rules. If everyone did the same, took the initiative and listened to their own inner voice, the welfare state would be certain of success. It would be updated. Man would rise above the despotism of machines and regulations.

The rabbit moved up to Vatanescu's collar.

Vatanescu pushed it back inside his shirt.

Usko Rautee asked what it was.

Nothing. Or rather, that is…

The rabbit moved round into the sleeve and from there jumped clumsily towards Rautee's desk. For a moment it clung to the edge of the desk by its front paws, and then, exerting all its energy, hauled up first its good hind-leg, and then the splinted one.

'It's a damned rat!'

The rabbit looked the employment officer in the eye. Rautee instinctively rolled back his chair. Vatanescu dived after the rabbit and tried to catch it in his hands. The animal hopped off the desk into Rautee's lap, and Rautee threw it back on the desk again.

A harmless creature.

Don't be afraid.

The rabbit limped awkwardly across the desk with its splint, knocking over a penholder and Usko Rautee's water mug. The computer mouse fell to the floor, its base came off and the ball rolled along the carpet for several long seconds. With an embarrassed smile Vatanescu hurled himself after the rabbit. At last it came to a halt in the curtain hanging by the desk, which came adrift from its moorings and collapsed to the floor. The rabbit found Usko's eraser, popped it in its mouth and began to nibble it.

'Out! You're nothing but a horse trader! Out! I'll call the police.'

And all too soon the siren of a police car was heard outside. Vatanescu leapt down the stairs and managed to pass the front door just before the policemen got out of their car. He set off in the opposite direction, trying not to run to avoid drawing attention to himself.

I have international crime and the Finnish police after me.

I would cry if I wasn't laughing.

Ming Po had left Saigon for the Helsinki suburb of Malmi over thirty years earlier. His travel plans had been strongly influenced by the war, which had made it necessary for him and his family to seek exile abroad. They had rocked about in a mortally dangerous boat in the middle of the open sea, and had spent some of the time in refugee camps.

Ming's mother, Ding, had a magic spoon, as all good fairies do. She was like Finland's favourite television cook Teija Sopanen or Mother Amma before she took to embracing people. Outside there might be genocide, napalm or Noah's Flood, but within the confines of the tent or in the open air by a naked flame, the delicious fragrance of Ding Po's cooking always brought a smile to people's faces. The lack of raw materials was never a problem; Ding accepted difficult conditions as a challenge. Not only was she fond of cooking, but cooking was fond of her.

What casseroles Ding was able to simmer in the oven out of bamboo shoots and rat meat! She had the art of spice in her fingertips, the correct preparation times in her soul, and it could be said that for a whole decade her cooking had kept her family alive, both spiritually and physically. It soothed the horror of the everyday. Ding Po gave part of herself in every pot and bowl she served to her husband and children, of whom her favourite was Ming, who had preserved his chubby cheeks in spite of the hard times. He was Mum's kitchen companion, and he peeled onions at the age of three, gutted the burbot, plucked and jointed the pigeon, tasted the sauces and became an indisputable master of the balance between sweet and sour.

When their wandering as refugees ended in the autumn of 1977 in a well-heated two-room apartment in Malmi, Ding felt she had fulfilled her duty. She saw her three children asleep on a mattress on the floor, tested the central-heating radiator that distributed the warmth that came from afar, admired the electric cooker and oven in the kitchen, and went to put more blankets on her offspring.

Her husband, King Po, came to join her. He placed his hands on his wife's shoulders, and then Ding died. Having given everything, with the journey complete. With her children alive.

From his mother Ming Po inherited a wok and an attitude to life. You'll survive it all, never complain, see the good in people, you'll find it easier that way – of course they're stupid, but are you yourself so eternally wise? Think about that, look in the mirror, don't be proud and don't be cynical. They can take everything away from you, but don't let them have your cooking pot. A well-simmered casserole will open the way to anyone's heart. Be careful about what food you cook for which woman, and you will win them all. Listen to Pave Maijanen's record 'Take Care' when it comes out, then you will finally understand what I mean.

At the age of seventeen, Ming Po rented a disused fire station and set up a restaurant there. The restaurant became known as 'the Chinese restaurant', even though it had a carefully chosen Vietnamese name. In the queue at the local supermarket he met Marjatta, who became his wife. His father was against the marriage and wanted a daughter-in-law from his own people, but was talked round when Ming explained to him that the only girl who would meet his criteria was located thousands of miles away in a crisis zone. Ming said that Marjatta was just right for him, and, in particular, that she was also pregnant with his child. Mixed-race couples need the support of their families, not prejudices and misplaced pride. Papa King's objections finally ended when he met Marjatta's father Jorma. Jorma was in the glazing business in Vaasa, and he looked at the world from the same one-square-yard-sized plot of his native land as

King did. Like King, Jorma thought that everything was better in the old days, and that all the new places, objects, ideas, jobs, generations and music were characterised by an inexcusable laziness.

Ming cooked for the whole gang. How could one doubt a man whose Karelian hotpot melted in the mouth – or indeed deny him anything? Ming himself called it a Fhong Bain hotpot, after a recipe of his mother's, with the difference that in the Finnish version all the spices were left out. Ding had not written down any of her recipes, and Ming had inherited them by doing, watching and trying. In the same way he passed them on to his children, the eldest of whom was born in 1984 and received the name Ling Irmeli Po-Virtanen.

Ming's establishment was in competition with the Tillikka Restaurant, which served its schnitzels and herring sandwiches with beer to railway staff, librarians and people from the local engineering works. In the evenings they moved on to fortified wine and schnapps. Ming had followed his mother's instructions and adapted. He kept his restaurant open slightly later than the Tillikka and sold takeaway meals to people in a state of paralytic drunkenness. He also added schnitzel to his own menu. As soon as Ling Irmeli was three, Ming got her into the restaurant's kitchen and dining room. The little girl learned the trade from her father and became a customer attraction. No matter how frozen a nation may be, a small child always wins hearts. Even dictators don't use children only for propaganda purposes; they actually like them, for they provide a momentary relief from the planning of evil.

If the MasterChef format had been known in those days, Ming would have won the contest and received a boost to his career, but back then people preferred to watch comedy shows about rural police chiefs, and Ming had to take a longer road.

One cannot cheat in the matter of cuisine. Merely good is not good enough, but excellent always sells in the end. The price must not be too high, but the price of excellence must not be too low either. Ming bought his chickens, pork and beef from the Finnish countryside, caught his fish himself, learned how to hunt, adapted moose to his own style of cooking, set traps for hares in his back yard and taught himself how to use all those edible plants that grow in the Finnish forest, but which the Finns had forgotten about since the 1750s. Ming used no artificial flavourings, because he had at his disposal the flavourings he inherited from his mother: love, daring, knowledge, courage, passion, and the ability to deal with failure.

In the mid-1980s the Malmi restaurant began to make a profit. In January 1989 some skinheads in pilot jackets smashed the window with an oar, but the next time they tried the same trick Ming invited them in and suggested they sample a bamboo leaf boat and a bowl of sweet-and-sour beef before they engaged in any more acts of vandalism and violence. If they could say in all honesty that it tasted bad, they could go ahead and throw their oar. Kick the asylum seekers to hell, as their slogan said. Pete, Miksu and Tumppi sampled the beef. It made their hair grow. The lads repaired the window and found summer jobs in Ming's restaurant.

Ming escaped xenophobia, but to cope with the economic downturn he had only the same weapons as his neighbours. A pint of lager for ten Finnish marks. To that, too, Ming adapted, hanging up his mother's wok on the wall and waiting beside his beer tap for the day when people would be hungry again and not thirsty all the time.

On the day that ice hockey star Ville Peltonen scored three goals and Ming's restaurant was filled with men in pilot jackets watching it on the ceiling-mounted TV, the wind changed. By the following Monday the shares in ethnic restaurants were rivalling those of Nokia. They were called ethnic, though Ming considered himself more of a resident of Malmi than of Vietnam. His children, born in Finland, spoke two languages but were of one mind.

People came all the way from downtown Helsinki to sample Ming's cookery, so he took the risk and moved his restaurant to a more expensive location closer to where the majority of his customers lived, and even started another, entrusting its management to his daughter. It was now twenty years since he first arrived in Finland, and during all that time he had slept no more than seven and a half hours a night. His resting pulse rate was one hundred and sixty.

The cornerstone of the downtown restaurant became a reasonably priced and plentiful lunch buffet, because that was what Finns liked. You paid a finite amount of cash and received an infinite amount of food. Not that you were able to stuff yourself infinitely, but there had to be freedom. Freedom with the corn and the peas at the salad bar, freedom to take an enormous mound of sausages and ketchup. During their lunch hour Ming served them his own idea of fusion cuisine: in addition to Asian dishes there were Hanoi Grandma's meatballs and especially Finland's staple food, the pizza. The Ho Chi Bling-Bling – with a combination of ham, kebab, chicken wings and pepperoni – was the favourite among the young. You could also get it on a rye base, for the more adult taste.

Vatanescu sat down at a window table that some people from the advertising agency Kr-öm & co had just vacated. He saw the reflection of his face in the window: a bearded, empty, squeezed-dry mug.

Instil confidence with the banknotes, dispel suspicion.

Ling Irmeli Po-Virtanen handed him the menu and inquired if the gentleman would like something to drink.

Vatanescu asked for water, and drank it in great gulps. He kept a constant eye on the door, fearing the arrival of the lady from the health centre, the man from the employment agency, the Russo-Balkan mafia and the Finnish police. When he put his glass down on the table, the rabbit hobbled out of his sleeve towards the spice rack.

Ling Irmeli politely backed away.

We won't hide any more. With Yegor's money I'll buy us an hour of peace.

Vatanescu scratched the rabbit under its chin, the place where all animals and humans go limp with satisfaction, because it means acceptance. It gets rid of anger, stress and aggression.

Who would scratch me under my chin?

Ling Irmeli told her father what she had seen. Ming looked from the kitchen into the restaurant and saw Vatanescu studying the menu, saw the rabbit sniffing the salt and pepper shakers. Ming recognised the type: a refugee, an asylum seeker. The best thing for him would be a seven-course dinner with flavour and substance, a blend of cultures, a dash of aesthetics and some nice surprises. He told his daughter not to complain about what the customer had brought in with him, as long as it wasn't leprosy or a suicide bomb. If here people ate pigs, oxen and bamboo shoots hauled from the other end of the earth, there was room for a paying rabbit. In old Ding's home village the animals lived together with the human beings under the same roof, because they needed one another.

That was what Vatanescu got, real food. A spring roll wrapped in a slice of pizza. Soy sauce, curry sauce, chilli sauce, sweet-and-sour chicken, sweet-and-sour pork, Karelian hotpot in chilli sauce. The rabbit nibbled three platefuls of salad, drank one bowl of milk after another and settled down to sleep on Vatanescu's lap. And that was no wonder, what with the first proper meal of its life in its belly, or what belly a rabbit has.

Vatanescu looked at the people in the restaurant. There were white-collar workers, there was the creative group, there was the depressed group, there were pensioners from the suburb of Myllypuro who had heard about the tasty, satisfying and reasonably priced lunch. There were yellow-helmeted building workers and there was Miihkali Toropainen with his family, considering divorce.

The boy is blowing bubbles in his Coca-Cola.

The girl is twirling a noodle on her chopstick with her fingers.

What's my son doing at this moment?

Vatanescu ordered coffee with dessert and helped himself to a triple portion of fruit salad, putting aside the pieces of peach, which the rabbit sucked in the human way.

Everything is going really well for us today.

We're going to take a room at a hotel, the kind of hotel that has bathrobes. Tomorrow morning I'll go back and see the man at the employment agency again. He promised us a roof over our heads. He was more good than bad.

Vatanescu paid Ling Irmeli with Yegor's banknotes

and told her to keep the change. He asked for two plastic bags to take away the uneaten food, and the salad for the rabbit. One doesn't throw good things away.

One doesn't throw bad things away, either.

As he stood between the rice pan and the grill, Ming examined the banknote his daughter had brought him. Right, clearly a proper forgery. He said he would take care of the matter and went to Vatanescu's table. Vatanescu was stroking the rabbit and blowing out his cheeks with satisfaction, his stomach replete. But Ming did not know how to be hard, was incapable of issuing a brutal demand. The customer had clearly enjoyed his cooking.

Ming had never given orders to his children; he preferred to be silent. He had learned this first from his father, and then from his neighbour Seppo Mäkäräinen. He did not like to talk about money because his world was all about food. He didn't really want to speak at all, for one could express all the things one needed to express by means of cookery. Love, anger, happiness in one's grandchildren, one's thoughts and emotions. Rather than to other chefs, Ming compared himself to a painter or a sculptor.

And yet.

A ragamuffin and a rabbit had paid with a three-hundred-euro banknote, and there was no such thing in this world. Did they think he was stupid? Ought he to call the police?

I could call them, but I won't. That was how Ming began his speech to Vatanescu, after standing before him for several minutes. Continuing, Ming said he was a stubborn small businessman who had to pay an exorbitant rent that was the equivalent of wages for five people, and it would be nice to be able to get some sleep occasionally. Sometimes it might even be nice to pay himself a wage. That was why childish tricks played by adults merely provoked him.

Vatanescu told Ming in English that he didn't understand Chinese, or was it Cantonese or Mandarin.

Ling Irmeli came over to translate her father's speech, and thus a degree of understanding began to develop.

I didn't know that it was… Of course it was forged. It came from Yegor, that money. The whole man is a forgery. The owner of an object transmits his karma to it, that's what old Gurda used to say. I'm still broke, and my son has no football boots.

'Bloody hell!' Ming said.

They were the first swearwords Ming Po had uttered in his life. The whole restaurant turned round to look at him. Someone applauded in astonishment, like at school when some sixth-former drops a glass of milk on the floor and they have to live it down for the rest of the year.

'Rabbit man! Do not lie to me. The easiest thing is to tell the truth!'

I know.

At least life has taught me that.

Ming gradually became himself again by some sort of continuous speed control. He remembered his mother's teachings. The customer is always right. A good deed is never lost. Vatanescu deserved a show of mercy, particularly as his eyes shone with a sincerity in which there was no stupidity.

When the lunchtime rush hour gave way to a moment of peace, Vatanescu found himself beside a man-sized pile of clean plates, glasses, cutlery and saucepans. He had paid for his meal by washing dishes.

Ming invited Vatanescu into his office. Vatanescu picked up his rabbit and tried to slip away, but Ming pointed to the chair, and Vatanescu sat down.

On the wall there were framed photographs of Ding Po and Ming's favourite Finnish female artiste, Meiju Suvas. The two women bore a distinct resemblance to each other, and Meiju Suvas had a dish named after her on the menu. It was Ming's dream to have her sing in the restaurant on his fiftieth birthday next summer. At least one song, at least 'Come Bite Me!'. On the other hand, he was not sure whether he really wanted to organise a party; there was too much work to do. And anyway, Ming did not like the idea of being the centre of attention.

Ming told Vatanescu that he was not interested in his past, but had a slight impression that his future was shrouded in darkness. Vatanescu nodded.

I want a job.

Give me a job.

Pay me what you like.

My son will have his football boots.

As if in answer to Vatanescu's thoughts, Ming said that he would willingly employ someone so keen to work, but Finland's social security and pension costs were so high that a small business owner could only hope to hire additional labour in his dreams, and so is forced to do all the extra work himself. He didn't want to employ black-market labour either, because if he did that his licence would be revoked, and with it his livelihood.

I guessed it.

Ming showed him the photograph of a range of Lapland fells that hung between the portraits of his mother and Meiju Suvas. If Vatanescu wanted to be the master of his own destiny, he would need to go to Lapland.

Ming spoke of the wide open spaces, the marshes and the south-facing slopes where marketable natural riches grew. Bilberries and lingonberries and especially cloudberries – so-called 'yellow gold'. If Vatanescu wanted real banknotes instead of forged ones, if he was not afraid of work, if he needed some quick wages for himself and his rabbit, then berry-picking was the job for him.

Ming showed him in a guide which berries and mushrooms were worth picking, which ones showed the best return. Then Ming told him about everyman's right, a right that was shared by Romanian and Vietnamese everymen, too. In the early 1990s Ming had often done berry- and mushroom-picking. The contents of those red and blue buckets had paid several income tax bills and the interest on several loans.

Vatanescu thumbed through the guide, in which the section on cloudberries was marked with a paperclip. Ming told him that Finns preferred to buy frozen Swedish berries rather than pick them for themselves. It made no sense, in the same way that, although Finland had thousands of lakes, instead of buying pike perch Finns bought fillets of panga from the fishrearing tanks of Ming's homeland. Berry-picking was like prospecting for gold: only the most grabbing guerrillas succeeded, and then not always, but everyone had the chance. You didn't need to speak the language, you didn't need any training, and no work permits were required.

Ming opened a wardrobe and showed Vatanescu a black suit, a white shirt, a tie and a pair of polished shoes. The suits were meant for waiters, but the largest size had never been used.

Ling Irmeli translated her father's words:

'Smarten yourself up; you can sleep on the kitchen floor. We'll look up the Lapland train times on the World Wide Web. You'll be leaving tomorrow.'

From his desk drawer Ming produced a razor and a can of shaving cream, which he gave to Vatanescu.

The next phase in the development of his bundle of old clothes would soon be lice, then rot. Vatanescu threw the bundle into the rubbish bin and closed the lid tight.

He stood naked before the mirror in the basement toilet. His hair was unkempt, his beard straggling, the dirt came off his face on his fingertips. In a dictionary he would have been found under the entry for 'pariah'. He seized his beard and used scissors to cut it all back to a half-inch in length, letting the tangled hairs float down into the washbasin. Then he squeezed some shaving foam onto the palm of his hand and spread it on his cheeks, his jaw and upper lip. He shaved his chin with rasping strokes. As the stubble disappeared, a new man emerged. Next Vatanescu cut his hair, and little by little his ears, his forehead and the nape of his neck were exposed.

Outward appearance sorted.

Is my outward life also going to be sorted?

He rinsed his face and armpits with water, dampened the hand towels and rubbed himself down all over. A brownish liquid flowed from the towels into the drain. Vatanescu cut his fingernails and four hairs that were growing on his earlobe. He looked at himself.

Who are you?

Vatanescu looked at himself from the side.

Who are you?

Vatanescu leaned very close to the mirror. His eyes were bloodshot, red, black and yellow, as though they were being tested in some medical experiment.

Where am I going?

What can a person freely decide for himself?

Vatanescu removed the white shirt from its hanger.

The last time I wore a suit was at my wedding. Or was it at Miklos's christening?

He buttoned the shirt, got his legs into the trousers. There weren't enough holes in the belt, so he pierced some more with the scissors.

I'm not a pariah any more. What am I?

Vatanescu pulled on the suit jacket and sat on the lavatory in order to tie the shoelaces. The bathroom mirror showed him the familiar eyes and a very, very faint smile. A big step forward from the deadly fear he had felt the day before, and after his flight from the police that morning. He took a deep breath and opened the door of the toilet, then made his way upstairs to the restaurant.

The shoes tapped on the wooden stairs in a dignified way. It was a sound quite different from the flopping of his old slip-on trainers, which had said, I'm going where I'm good enough to go. The new shoes said that this man knew where he was going and was travelling business class.

When he arrived at the doorway of the restaurant, Vatanescu saw a sight that filled him with horror. Ling Irmeli was talking to two policemen. They were holding a photograph of Vatanescu. Once again he took flight – though this time it was his mind that fled, for he remained standing where he was. There were two possibilities. He could go back to the toilet and lock himself in. That would mean arrest. Or he could do what he always had to do. Run away.

Do you remember who looked at you in the mirror just now?

A new man, a different man, everyman.

I'm not the man who was washing dishes in the restaurant kitchen a moment ago.

Vatanescu looked at his reflection in the tall window.

I'm not a pariah. I don't hug the wall. I walk straight.

I'm not the person they are looking for.

They aren't looking for me.

And so Vatanescu, running a risk of one hundred per cent with a self-confidence of seventy, strode calmly behind Ling Irmeli and crossed the restaurant to the kitchen, right in front of the policemen's faces.

Ming greeted him in the kitchen doorway with a train timetable in his hand. He had seen the policemen arrive and had told his daughter to distract them for a while. Vatanescu needed only to climb out of the window onto the bin for old newspapers and from there head out through the courtyard. Once he was in the street it was only a few hundred yards to the railway station.

Without further thought, Vatanescu jumped out of the window. It was only when he had already broken into a run that he remembered the rabbit.

Ming whistled from the window.

Vatanescu caught the rabbit like a ball.

Hey ho, let's go.

Chapter Five

In which Vatanescu gravitates to first class, smokes a joint and finds a Volvo.

Vatanescu sat down on the only vacant seat in the carriage and kept his gaze fixed on the floor.

A beggar doesn't achieve his goals.

A beggar doesn't get berries or football boots for his son.

Change yourself.

Vatanescu perceived himself as an outsider. He watched the other passengers in suits and shoes that clicked. The best of them wore their uniform in a relaxed but confident way. They demanded a treatment that fitted their status, and got it. They had laptop computers, touchscreen mobile phones and very thin wallets, just a few plastic cards. Thus the world changes. Nowadays a fat wallet was the mark of an obsessive collector of receipts, where once it meant having enough cash to buy the world. These men could buy the world and only needed two cards to manage their lives.

Try to look like them, then you'll gain entry to first class, you'll be the owner of an iPad.

Three teenagers were sitting at Vatanescu's table. Children to his eyes, adults in theirs. One of them was Jonttu, a grammar-school graduate and former ice hockey prospect dressed in a casual style, who liked others to laugh at his jokes, though not at him. His father wanted him to carry on in his glazing business, which interested Jonttu even less than the course at a vocational training school which his mother hoped he would take.

The Beggar & the Hare

At Jonttu's age the meaning of life was freedom, in all its forms. The price of this was an empty soul, empty words and an empty bank account. But today, like his travelling companions Ökö and Minttu, he had a clear goal: a job in an ore mine, and the hourly wage of more than twenty euros that was paid there.

Vatanescu greeted the teens with a nod and took a sip of water.

Try to look like a man in a suit.

Talk like a man in a suit.

Invent a life for yourself.

Under his arm the rabbit nibbled some carrot.

Having looked at the railway timetable and the list of fares, Vatanescu decided that his journey would have to end no later than the third stop unless he was able to find some more money. He checked the pockets of his jacket and trousers as though there ought to be something there which had now gone. For this, an expression of genuine surprise was needed, as it was even harder to lie with gestures than with words.

Ökö, a first-year student of tourism and a consumer of cannabis products, surveyed the foreigner who sat opposite. The foreigner's plastic bags smelled mouth-wateringly good – precisely the kind of Chinese food that tastes so delicious after one has smoked a couple of grams of hash.

What does a man in a suit do if his wallet and phone have been stolen?

Vatanescu twitched and shrugged his shoulders, spread his hands and waited for one of the teenagers to ask what the trouble was. The first to react was Minttu, Jonttu's classmate and possibly his girlfriend. (It wasn't clear, because Minttu wasn't sure whether she liked Jonttu or Ökö, or even whether in general she preferred girls or boys. Why, in the course of the same year, did you have to be able to decide on the colour of your hair, your sexual orientation, your field of study, your attitude to life and which political party to vote for? A year in an ore mine would help you make decisions about your life, things that right now you change your mind about three times a day.)

'Something wrong?'

Vatanescu cleared his throat, swallowed and was unable to tell a lie.

Stay close to the truth. Vary it.

Vatanescu said he had lost his bank card, relying on the memory of losing a postcard in Timisoara in 2002. He said that his mobile phone had also disappeared, and indeed it had, as he had sold it to Yegor in exchange for a pack of oat-flakes.

Get into the swing of it, choose the right words, loads of conviction.

Put in a twist at the end.

Vatanescu asked when the ticket collector would be along. He couldn't get off at an interim station to find out because he had business waiting for him in Lapland and there weren't any more flights that day. Ökö said that the ticket collector usually came round before Tikkurila, in about fifteen minutes' time.

Keep calm. Don't force it. Don't cause tensions.

Vatanescu asked the teenagers where they were going.

Jonttu's map showed all the mining areas, and planned mining areas, across Finland and Sweden. He had also printed out a bundle of information – maps, data, company profiles – and firmly believed that if he did not succeed on the first attempt, then surely by the third he would. There must be plenty of work there for those who looked for it. Vatanescu took from his pocket the map of the national park that Ming had given him, and pointed to his own destination.

The right words. The details.

Vatanescu put his finger on a circle. The area inside it was said to contain peat bogs that produced the highest yield of cloudberries.

Raw material trading.

Vatanescu's destination was close to where the teenagers were going, and his ultimate aims were not so distant from theirs either.

Natural riches, preliminary explorations.

'In the area of the national park?'

All over the place. If I find what I'm looking for, nothing will get in my way.

The teenagers looked at the smooth-shaven man in a suit sitting in front of them, and then at one another.

'What do they have up there? Gold?'

'Diamonds?'

'Oil?'

Yellow stuff. Valuable stuff.

They asked what company Vatanescu represented, what his position was.

They'll catch you out if you mention names or describe things in too much detail.

Remember the men in suits. In first class.

Just tell them the essentials. But don't lie so you don't have to explain. Explaining is what will get you caught.

Vatanescu said that he worked for himself. He sold outputs, results and reports to the highest bidder. Thus he was able to make the quick decisions that in large businesses can take months. And he knew where to invest his profits. In the future, in future generations.

In football boots.

He said he had started out in the financial sector but had discovered new challenges in the raw material market.

Jonttu wanted to know from Vatanescu what the advantages were of working in mines with regard to wages and conditions of employment. Minttu was interested in whether women were able to take jobs as drivers of forklift trucks or ore transport lorries.

Everything is possible. You have excellent backgrounds and the hourly rate is so high that... er... a Romanian beggar... could live for a whole year on a month's wages.

The teenagers thought the comparison was far-fetched, but they liked what he told them.

It's also OK to smile while you're working. You can look other people in the eye, even if those eyes are blackened by coal. There's always some white flashing in them.

The train stopped at Pasila.

Listen...

Vatanescu's words stuck in his throat. To request a loan was risky, especially if he was asked about his credit record, which was worse than that of Greece. It could all collapse, it was all useless.

Well, anyway...

The express train sped through Malmi without stopping, then Tapanila. After Puistola it began to slow down as it approached Tikkurila. The teenagers chatted together in Finnish. They laughed at all sorts of things, as kids do at that age – laugh and be sceptical.

Act. Act now.

The train stopped.

What am I going to do?

The rabbit slipped out of his sleeve onto the seat and then to the floor. From there it climbed up beside the teenagers.

It sat on Ökö's lap, and encountered no resistance. In a flash their astonishment turned into affection. The rabbit looked at the teenagers and by its demeanour permitted them to stroke it.

Jonttu took photos with his camera phone and they asked why the head of an investment company was travelling with a rabbit.

'Are you a magician?'

It's like a… canary. In a mine. Life insurance. It detects danger. Sniffs out precious metals. Only eight rabbits in the world are specially trained like it.

Vatanescu lay on one of the upper berths in the four-berth sleeping compartment. The berth had been intended for Oili Tymäkkä, who had not received her parents' permission to go and work in a mine for a year because they had already paid for her to take a cramming course in legal studies.

Vatanescu looked at the ceiling and listened to the delight of the teenagers as they fondled and fed the rabbit.

Just before the train arrived in Seinäjoki, Jonttu dug from his wallet a brown lump, which he crumbled onto cigarette paper with some powdered tobacco.

'Feel like a smoke?'

I don't smoke.

'Just a puff or two.'

I must be worthy of their trust. They mean well.

I mustn't be arrogant.

At first the joint made Vatanescu smile. Then he felt as though he had floated in through the door, along the corridors into the sleeping compartment and lain down on a bed. Then he felt terribly hungry. Then Jonttu went off to the restaurant car to buy something that would stave off the hunger. Then Vatanescu's tongue began to loosen.

The biggest problems in the labour market are caused by management structure and working conditions. There's a need for the workforce to feel that they are wanted and secure. That's how a spirit of solidarity is built. There must be barbecues now and then. We need to feel that we're important, that's all. That we can have an influence on the way things are run, and that we're taken notice of and listened to. These are things that don't have much to do with the world of finance, but the problem is that no one ever asks any questions. Think. We need to think about things and not just chase the money. Yet that is what I do, and what you do. I don't know. It's something that needs to be given thought.

Minttu, who was taking notes with her Stabilo pen, underlined the word 'barbecue' in three different colours.

Profit-sharing is essential, twenty-five per cent is not enough. Those who make the greatest physical effort must receive adequate remuneration for putting the strength of their bodies at the company's disposal. Prostitution and human trafficking are combated, but no one objects to the fact that building workers also sell their bodies. The management swindles its subordinates, lines its own pockets and cuts back on toilet breaks. Think about it.

Jonttu returned with eight bags of potato crisps, which they mixed with the delicacies Vatanescu had brought from Ming's restaurant. They ate like pigs and played the board game 'Star of Africa' like children. Vatanescu amassed the biggest fortune in emeralds and rubies, but lost it to a robber in Madagascar.

How can one person take from another the money he has earned with his labour and then enjoy an untroubled night's sleep?

They drank Coca-Cola and the cider the teenagers had brought with them, and in the next game Vatanescu made do with being the banker.

In this game all the players start off with three hundred pounds. In real life many people start off with little more than hunger and a pair of leaky shoes. Should it be like that? Must think about it. Could it be different? Is money the solution?

I'm going to lie here and think.

Vatanescu's mind and body were mellow, gentle, floating. He looked out of the window; the view out there was still the same, little stations, housing estates and industrial parks shortly before and after the main stops. Forest and more forest, becoming less and less tall the further north they went.

With a start, on the border between sleeping and waking, Vatanescu once again saw the eve of his departure from Romania. His son had dozed off between the wall and his grandmother, whose lungs were as ravaged by damp as the wallpaper. He could still save his son; an eight-year-old boy could recover from almost anything as long as he had fruit juice and football boots. His son's joy in life was still strong, despite the attempts of older boys to get him to sniff glue with them. Vatanescu had lit the stove, fetched more firewood from the outside wall. He had noticed his mother watching him and asked what the matter was. His mother had said she knew that tomorrow her son would be leaving.

'Will you be able to endure what will come?'

'What will come?' Vatanescu had asked.

'Anything can come.'

'I'm doing it for you.'

Vatanescu then went off to bed, but could not sleep, and waited for the morning. The new day was waiting there, too.

That's how days are. They arrive and we don't know what they will bring. Or what we are allowed to take from them.

Have Yegor's men come to the village? Will they be looking for my son? Am I that valuable to them?

These young people have left their parents in order to live their own lives.

I left my son.

How would one describe Finnish Lapland to a foreign reader, to one from Germany, for example? Would one describe the shaman drums? The noise of building work? The Sami costumes? The Russian four-by-fours, the drunken British tourists and the Finnish screen actors? The Dutch motor sledge safari groups, cheeks red with the cold, smiling broad smiles after extreme experiences? The Crazy Reindeer Hotel, with its concerts by entertainers like Popeda or Paula Koivuniemi and the business travellers copulating in the cheapest rooms? The reindeer, both the live ones and those that have been turned into steaks and processed meat? One might describe all of those things, but now the train is clanking into its destination, drawn by proper old Soviet locomotives with diesel engines handed down from grandfathers to grandsons.

Vatanescu stood on the platform of the last station in this small country, more than six hundred miles to the north of the point where the train had begun its journey. The teenagers gave him the winter clothes that had been intended for the fourth passenger, as well as a pointed woollen cap and sling for the rabbit, both knitted by Jonttu.

Vatanescu pulled the quilted jacket over his suit and put on the thermal boots. He promised to reimburse the teenagers for all the help they had given him, took down the numbers of their bank accounts and wished them all the best for their future lives. From the sling the rabbit showed a paw, which the teenagers shook one by one.

Children, appreciate all that you have the chance to acquire.

The teenagers continued their journey by taxi. From his inside pocket Vatanescu took the guide that Ming had given him and found the section on berries.

Third-generation railwayman Mikko Maukas was unloading cars from the night express. Each year they increased in size, enormous SUVs with tiny female drivers who wore immaculate makeup. Number plates from every country in Europe. Professional builders who had gone south to Estonia to buy cheaper ceiling panels. Maukas was used to tourists from Finland and abroad, their automatic gearboxes, their questions. Were there reindeer here? Could one use pounds and dollars? Could one take reindeer on board trains or planes? Was it all right to shoot them? Why didn't anyone speak French? His reply was the smile that men in Lapland are given at birth, a smile that can mean anything from vitriolic abuse to falling in love. Up from the station trudged yet another tourist or businessman dressed in arctic gear, carrying two plastic bags. Sometimes they even tried to look poor, especially the wealthiest ones, like that furniture magnate Kamppari or whatever his name was, Maukas thought.

Vatanescu asked where he could find lingonberries and bilberries. Mikko Maukas looked at the investor, who did not fit his idea of a berry-picker. Why was the fellow talking in metaphors, why should an unloader of cars have to know all the features of different cultures?

Berry-pickers were either Flips or Russkies. That wasn't racism, Mikko said to himself; those words were just easier to say than Filipinos and Ukrainians; the guys who arrived in minivans wearing the same kind of tracksuits that Mikko wore in summer. On the other hand, investor types like the man who was standing in front of him were usually picked up at Kittilä Airport by his taxi-driver brother who then drove them around the mining zones past, present and future. If you wanted a decent tip you had to supply them with an Internet connection, a teardrop-shaped bottle of mineral water and a phone charger with a bunch of different USB connectors.

Mikko Maukas asked Vatanescu which car on the car transporter was his. Was it the Volvo XC90, the thing that looked like a heffalump, quite unsuitable for city driving, with a ride height far too low to be a real off-roader? But then, if he had the money to boost his ego with something like that, why not?

No, berries. So I can buy football boots.

Mikko Maukas drove the silver-coloured SUV into the car park, left the engine running and got Vatanescu to sign the delivery form. Vatanescu said nothing. He got into the driver's seat.

Under the seat were settings for lumbar, posterior and soul. The radio played gentle noonday classical music, and the logbook of the vehicle's real owner was in the glove compartment. Thomas Weissbier of Gothenburg. This meant that Vatanescu would soon have international crime, the Finnish police and the Swedish upper middle class on his heels.

For a moment he studied the automatic gearbox, then found D and drove the vehicle out of the car park. It would be more than an hour before Thomas Weissbier was woken in his sleeping compartment on the train.

Vatanescu drove along the quiet road in the big vehicle, surveying the low houses, the sparsely inhabited neighbourhoods. Absolutely everywhere in this country – in the cities, the medium-sized towns, the villages – grocery stores faced you in twos, one on each side of the street. The name of one began with an S, the other with a K, the difference in prices visible in the way the customers were dressed. Fur coats for the K, windcheaters and rubber boots for the S. The only exceptions were the agricultural workers, who patronised the K, for which they supplied most of the produce. The service stations were marked by towers as tall as minarets, and the cars that stopped at the petrol pumps were, surprisingly, tough old Japanese ones. However, just at that moment Vatanescu's Swedish Volvo passed a queue of German luxury cars that were being tested in these northern conditions. When the Swedish satnav told him he had travelled *åttiosju kilometer* (eighty-seven kilometres) a police car came along in the opposite direction. It didn't stop, but Vatanescu had the impression that it at least slowed down, and heads turned round.

I'm not a thief.
I'm a berry-picker.

Chapter Six

In which Vatanescu takes a sauna and drinks with Harri Pykström

Vatanescu's example had encouraged the remaining beggars to defend their rights, or rather develop them for themselves. Under Balthazar's leadership they rose up in revolt against the low pay and poor working conditions. Yegor Kugar knew how to put down a revolt in a crisis zone or in fledgling democracies, but in a Nordic state where the rule of law prevailed it was impossible to use weapons, hooded men or even waterboarding.

The balance of power was reversed. That always comes as a happy surprise to the subordinates and as a shock to whoever has been giving the orders and doing the subordinating. Yegor's astonishment is expressed very well in his own words:

'A) How can people be so ugly? B) How can people be so unpleasant? C) How can people be so stupid? D) How the devil can I be even more stupid?

'Begging. A major flop. I'd have made more money if I'd stood on a street corner strumming "Smoke on the Water" on a balalaika.

'The gypsy campers grumbled, played tricks, failed to declare their earnings, started claiming mileage allowances. Some of them went back home, and each of those quite definitely left their debts unpaid. To the bunch that remained Vatanescu had become a kind of Che Guevara. The same guys who previously hadn't dared to look me in the eye were playing the game of October Revolution.'

It was a change of authority, but above all it was an evaporation of authority. Vatanescu's surprise attack had knocked Yegor Kugar to the floor and the referee had counted to ten. A technical knockout, nose out of joint, four years' sick leave, if he was entitled to it.

The banknotes Vatanescu had taken from Yegor Kugar were fakes, but what really mattered was that, with them, he had taken the man's authority. When Yegor Kugar's authority evaporated, his genuine banknotes evaporated too. He wanted to go and get Vatanescu back, but the Organisation refused its support. While Yegor felt that he had been let down, the Organisation felt that he had let them down. He had failed at his job; the structural change had gone in the wrong direction.

'Vatanescu had vanished like a fart down Station Tunnel in October. And I didn't think I'd be able to find one of the lowliest losers in this world on my own.'

The reindeer fixed Vatanescu with a placid, cow-like stare, but this new arrival made no more impression on them than all the previous arrivals who for centuries had come to Lapland to assert their everyman's right. He was just another of them, the academics on skis, the Dutch motor sledge safari groups; the military patrollers and the pop stars on the slalom slopes.

Vatanescu set off on foot through the marshy terrain until he sank up to his knees and had to climb to drier ground. He did not stop until he reached the summit of a fell, facing a cairn to which every previous backpacker had added a stone, large or small. He put a small stone on top of the others.

Then he sat down on a flat rock and scooped the rabbit out of its sling and onto his lap. Together they surveyed the world that stretched away for dozens of miles.

Have you ever known such silence? Have you ever been away from people, away from the fear of their reactions?

Three hundred and sixty degrees of fells, lakes and bogs. True, here and there the landscape was broken by the hotels of the skiing centres, by lifts, cranes and 3G network sites.

I'm not afraid.

It's strange.

But I'm not afraid.

That lemming there couldn't care less where I'm from, or how I earn my money, as long as I don't step between him and his young. Or on him. Round hills, old reindeer enclosures, this is all like the cottage of Komar Tudos back home. It never changes, even though everything else does.

Some part of us is always the same, no matter who we are. Fate, chance, the sperm of our fathers and the ova of our mothers determine the course of our lives. In a way that is senseless, unanswerable, ineluctable. One person's place is in Finland, another's in Romania, yet another's in Hollywood.

On a foreign, unknown soil I'm free.

Penury is not a prison. Nor are hunger or poverty. It's people. The haves in relation to the have-nots. The owners protecting their property. Of course.

I protect you, my rabbit, but I don't own you.

We are brothers.

Vatanescu and the rabbit continued their journey along the chain of fells, down, up, down, up. After hours of walking his legs began to find the right footholds by themselves, without looking. The tiredness helped; as he no longer had the strength to correct his mistakes, it was better not to make them. As a result he was able to look several yards ahead instead of focusing solely on his toes.

On the evening of the second day Vatanescu set the rabbit free.

One day I will have to let my son go into the world, too.

To fail.

To succeed.

The rabbit had the cautious, clumsy and haughty step of a city-dweller, incapable of being instantly intoxicated by the wild rabbit it felt itself becoming. It adjusted the disproportionate muscles of its hind-legs to its own weight, tested its co-ordination, hopped like a claudicating drunkard on Hakaniemi Market Square. Time after time Vatanescu had to put it back on its paws again by lifting it up under its soft middle.

A step.

Another step.

Follow me, walk as I walk. Carefully, but blindly trusting in something.

There is only this moment. Yesterday we don't remember, tomorrow we don't know.

They reached a gorge between the fells, arriving at the edge of a marsh – and the edge was bursting with red and blue berries. Vatanescu picked them, putting the blue ones in the plastic bag with the S on it, and the red ones in the bag that was marked with a K. And before the onset of darkness, which here came late – or was it early? – he gathered wood to make a fire. On the scree of a fellside he found a level area bordered by three large rocks, and there he set up camp. A few unneeded pages of the nature guide lit the campfire; the book of matches bore the words 'Ming's Palace'. Then Vatanescu used his winter clothes to make a mattress, and his jacket to cover him.

The fire crackled, warming the stones beneath it and heating the last of the food he had brought from Ming's. Vatanescu put the white rice and the vegetables aside for the rabbit and let it drink milk from a carton. In the inside pocket of the suit jacket he found the sachets of instant coffee and sugar from the train, and when the rabbit had drained the milk carton he made the carton into a mug. Fresh water from the brook.

Before he fell asleep, Vatanescu looked up the section in the guide about the 'yellow gold' that Ming had mentioned. He showed the picture of the berry to the rabbit and told the rabbit to tug the legs of his trousers with its teeth if it saw any.

The beggar and the rabbit fell asleep under the starry sky on a bed of moss, content with themselves, their deeds and the reality that surrounded them.

In the basement of his home Harri Pykström was examining his video collection. Six shelves of Olympics, nature documentaries, Second World War documentaries, Clint Eastwood movies, Matti Ijäs movies, Edvin Laine movies, Westerns, the 1994 European Basketball Championships qualifying match between Finland and Ukraine and, the latest addition to his collection, the 2000 Four Hills Tournament between Germany and Austria. Rauni Mollberg's *Blessed Madness* and Mikko Niskanen's *Gotta Run!* were present on four different cassettes, because Harri Pykström taped those movies every time they were on TV.

Friday was Harri Pykström's video day, as were

Monday, Wednesday and Sunday. On this occasion he hesitated between *Inspection*, *The Wrestler* and *A Charming Mass Suicide*. Could one watch Ere Kokkonen's work while sober, or should the experience be left until the small hours, when drunkenness would give it the something extra it required? The films of Kokkonen, with their aggressive clarity and grinding narration, reminded Pykström of the training videos of his former employer, the Finnish army. Risto Jarva had a better understanding of the essence of humour. It wasn't jokes, but sorrow. Life was a tragic affair, where every minute took us closer to death. So one might as well laugh. Pykström was pleased with this idea, which had come to him, unprompted and unasked, after his heart attack. He had asked his wife Maija if she thought it a sign of psychological maturity or merely the result of upset mental equilibrium, a jolt, brain chemistry. All of those things, was Maija's reply. Just as his hand was reaching out for an Ijäs film, *Dolly and Her Lover*, Maija shouted that dinner was ready.

Pykström climbed the stairs, his knees cracking under the weight of his two hundred and seventy pounds of conviviality. He panted and puffed; they really should have had a lift put in when the house was renovated. Everything else had been done on his wife's initiative, which of course later became his own initiative as well.

Pykström raised the lid of the pan. Nothing could beat the aroma of a reindeer fry, except that of pipe tobacco or a freshly opened bottle of Calvados. Perhaps also salmon grilled on an open fire or, even better, trout. Pykström asked where the lingonberry jam was.

'Can't you see I'm doing my Zumba workout?'

Mrs Pykström wobbled on the living-room floor as

the female dance instructors wiggled on the television screen. Pykström looked at his wife, shovelled some reindeer fry and mashed potato onto a plate and then into his mouth. He thought of the nature documentaries in which the growth of plants is accelerated so that one can see the cycle of the seasons in thirty seconds. What would it be like, a speeded-up documentary that showed the onset of the fat on Mrs Pykström's back over all these twenty-three years? When they first met there had been a supple layer of flesh, where now her back and buttocks trembled like aspic. But Harri Pykström's back had a layer of flab that was just the same; indeed many couples who have lived together for a long time come to resemble one another in all sorts of respects. On the basis of the latest photos from Australia the same thing was also happening to their eldest son Jorma, who even in the maternity clinic had been called chubby first, and cheerful only second. Mrs Pykström attempted to get rid of her aspic by means of Zumba, Harri Pykström by means of oblivion.

He scraped the bottom of the pot of lingonberry jam and went to fetch a jar of pickled cucumbers from the pantry. A bright, tranquil evening. That was what was so wonderful here in Perä-Kompio: the quiet – no neighbours, no relatives, no music from the ice cream van, no surprise visitors. One's own bit of land, one's own peace, no damned berry-pickers talking about their pesky everyman's right.

Pykström ate three platefuls of dinner, belched and said thank you.

He switched on the coffeemaker. He sat down on the sofa, behind his wife. He said that the enthusiasm of the man who was jerking about on TV was due to the fact that he knew that fat old women all over the world were ordering his DVD. Why? Because they couldn't accept that they were getting old. In Harri Pykström's view all that wiggling would do no good when there were too many miles on the clock.

'Said the broken-down truck at the side of the road. You're just jealous.'

'True.'

Pykström finished his bottle of beer, got up and went to kiss Mrs Pykström on the neck. Of all the world's millions of Zumba dancers, this was the only one he loved. The aspic was the same resilient skin he had got to know and made his own in the early 1970s.

'Sweet-ass,' Pykström said, slapping his wife on the bottom.

Harri Pykström found it hard to talk about many things, but he expressed his loving feelings with the ease and swiftness of a child. They were sincere and true, and they had saved him many times. Pykström knew well that a man must have someone by his side, otherwise he would lose his place in the world. Otherwise he was done for.

Pykström poured himself a cup of coffee, adding some whole milk and four lumps of sugar, plus two which he put in his mouth. He took his camouflage jacket from the back of the door, checked that his cigarettes were in the front pocket and told his wife that he was going to heat the sauna, because he didn't feel in the mood this evening. As had been the case for years. Ever since his heart attack his interest had died, and Harri Pykström said he had moved from a focus on intercourse to the next phase of love. Banter.

Pykström put some logs in the basket, looked through the window and saw his wife wiping her forehead on her sponge bracelet. He wondered why he did not feel free, though he had arranged everything to that end.

He had early retirement, a cabin in Lapland, logs in his basket, a small-bore rifle just in case.

Once at the sauna Pykström made sure that his wife could not see him, and fetched a bottle from under the stone base. A little drop would be OK, a snort, a quick one, after all it was Friday night and there was a nice sunset. After the heart attack his doctor had forbidden him to drink, but they couldn't forbid you to live. On weekdays Pykström bought light beer on the Swedish side of the border more or less as a soft drink that didn't even give you a hangover. It made you slightly tipsy, and that would do.

He put some birch logs in the stove, tearing off some bark to act as kindling. His son had brought thirty-two cubic yards of dry birchwood in the truck and asked for the umpteenth time why he didn't have electricity installed. An electric sauna in a Lapland cabin? True, he felt a bit bad about using imported logs, but if he didn't have the strength to chop the firewood himself, then that was that. It was always the same story, thought Harri Pykström. There were too many things to make one's life easier, even though their original plan had been to live surrounded by nature on nature's terms, in the grip of wild beasts and the merciless elements. This reality had slapped him in the face like a wet rag, for nothing would prevent one from getting older, not even the realisation of a youthful dream.

Pykström sat down on the top bench of the sauna, listening to the crackle of the fire and the roar of the furnace. Perhaps just one more mouthful, perhaps just another swig, how could another little drop do him any harm?

That autumn it would be two years since the heart attack.

Harri Pykström had been applying for bail for a soldier who had gone AWOL, when his chest had exploded. On waking up in the recovery room, Harri Pykström knew that his new life was located in Perä-Kompio – where for several years now the Finnish army had had a cabin for sale, but he had lacked the courage, or the time, to buy it.

It was there that Pykström went. There that Pykström would die. At the end of a quad track, no mod cons, eighteen thousand euros, easy to look after.

'And what about me?' Mrs Pykström inquired with a cautious squawk.

'I won't go anywhere without you,' Pykström said.

'If you're planning to go somewhere in Lapland, you can go alone.'

Pykström packed his clothes, signed the deed of sale and flew to Kittilä. At a sports shop in Muonio he bought a quad bike, rode to the cabin and began to put it in order with an axe, a handsaw and a lot of motivation. But what could he hope to do, a man who weighed two hundred and seventy pounds and was recovering from a heart operation? He had had to use his satellite phone to call the emergency medical services helicopter, and resume his convalescence at Rovaniemi District Hospital.

Mrs Pykström had sworn at his hospital bedside that she would never again leave her fat, crazy husband alone, not even for an instant. Even Jorma, from Australia, expressed the modest hope that he would not immediately have to fly back again for the funeral. With his hand on the complete works of Arto Paasilinna, Harri Pykström promised to take things more easily.

Outside labour was hired to complete the repairs on

the house, and workmen came to the site all the way from Helsinki, Estonia and Norway. Pykström was looking for new ways to make money, and one of them was a plan to write short stories of the kind he had read as a young student in a flatshare, and had later liked to read while sitting on the toilet. As adjutant of a logistics company he had had to pound a typewriter every day, so even a whole novel might not have been out of his range. A wilderness novel for readers all over the Arctic region. He had told his wife that once the fibre optic cables had been installed on their property she ought to take a telecommuting job.

'You're crazy.'

Mrs Pykström had a degree in cultural anthropology and was working on a dissertation called *The World of Woman: Research Diaries from the World's Beginning to its Hypothetical End*. She promised to wait until the repairs were finished and then review the situation – perhaps here she would at last be able to complete her dissertation. Or at any rate she would have to wait until her crazy husband had recovered his senses.

Harri Pykström had attached a lifting apparatus to the trailer of his quad and helped the building workers to hoist the materials from the foot of the hill. He always did this stripped naked. When his wife asked him why, he replied that he was master in his own home and could do as he liked. This was nothing new to Mrs Pykström, for she had always treated her husband as an object of research: he possessed something in common with the men of the Huchu tribe studied by Bronislaw Malinowski, a tribe that cultivated a penis display ritual. Sincerity, bragging, a zest for life. Worship of wooden idols, self-elevation and self-abasement. How could one leave such a man? Leave him alone even for a few minutes?

When a man and a woman are fused together as a couple, they stay closer to each other than any pair of animals. An osmosis takes place in which one becomes a part of the other, no matter how different they are. Or even, in the view of outsiders, incompatible. Pykström and his wife loathed each other's respective hobbies of shooting and dancing in front of the television set; they loathed each other's favourite films. Harri Pykström had been sick only once in his life, when he saw his wife putting *Cocktail* on the video player. But this was precisely the basis of their love. When Harri Pykström called his wife a goddamn meatball, only Mrs Pykström knew what it really meant. My dear, my treasure. Come and warm the bed, let's make more children even though we're fifty, even though I have prostate trouble and you no longer have a uterus or ovaries. Mrs Pykström and Harri Pykström were aware of all these things; they had even discussed the matter and agreed about its old-fashioned sanctity. It was the sort of relationship that the young no longer understood at all, as they were too busy searching for themselves. The young were in quest of their own ego, their innermost being, and the best place to hold a rave-up. Instead they ought to be looking for someone. Someone to understand. Someone to support. Someone to love. Someone to make nice meals for, no matter how numbingly dreadful it was to share the same roof with them.

For telecommuting Mrs Pykström needed a broadband connection and more room for a study. Little by little the Pykström's cabin had become a modern private residence, which just happened to be situated in the middle of nowhere. Except that it wasn't in the middle of nowhere at all, for six miles away there was a skiing centre with more cultural, entertainment and sporting events than there had been in their old neighbourhood of Vantaa, next to Helsinki.

One morning Harri Pykström noticed he was living in a house that was identical in every respect to the one he had left, and again felt a stab in his chest. He had planned to spend his time fishing, hunting, living in harmony with nature, yet here he was riding to the village on his quad bike, buying the same Euro Shopper products as he could anywhere in Finland or Europe and sitting in the local pub to watch Premier League football. Pykström was not hermit material.

Pykström lit a fresh cigarette on the embers of the last one and opened another can of beer. The sauna thermometer read fifty-five degrees Celsius. He went outside to fetch more logs.

Vatanescu stopped by the edge of a narrow brook. He had already filled six plastic bags with berries and had taken them back to base camp. He was now on the last two, and found himself faced with a logistical problem. How were the bags to reach the customers?

The sweat trickled, the brook babbled, and Vatanescu wondered if it was all right to drink the water. When Panos Milos had drunk the water of the river in his home village he had grown a third arm, according to the story Panos's mother had told, at least. The rabbit jumped onto a stone in the middle of the brook and lapped some water with its tongue.

Then Vatanescu drank, too, and the water tasted better than his first bottle of Coca-Cola in the summer of 1990, with Maria on the bridge of the ancient ruined city of Stenea. Vatanescu splashed water on his face and dried his hands on the hem of his shirt. The white collared shirt had turned black with the juice of the berries, as had his hands. When he raised his eyes, on the other side of the brook he saw a small building. Bending down in front of it was a naked man built like a barrel.

Are there people here? What should I say to him?
What do people like? Be honest.

Vatanescu waved his hand, and shouted that he was an everyman.

Harri Pykström had just finished putting the logs in the basket when he saw someone gesturing to him from the other side of the brook. On his land, on one of his sauna evenings, it was hardly likely to be a surveyor. A man with black hair, wearing a quilted jacket. The man looked like a Sicilian, or maybe even a terrorist. At the stage of intoxication that Pykström had reached any kind of emotional reaction was possible, and he chose fear. It took the outward form of anger. Filthy invaders, he thought. He also reflected that if they were on one's own private land it was all right to shoot them, and went to get his small-bore rifle from the sauna changing room. The rifle was meant for shooting willow grouse and other small game, but could also be used to repel attacks by foreign invaders.

The man was still waving on the other side of the brook when Pykström got down on one knee and took aim. The man was holding something white, and some creature was jumping around at his feet. Pykström pulled the trigger.

Vatanescu threw himself flat on his face at the edge of the brook. The water zipped around him four more times, and then there was silence. He kept his head underwater, like a small child who hides his eyes and thinks no one can see him.

Pykström stampeded across the rocky ground towards the brook and told Vatanescu to get up.

Though Vatanescu did not understand what Pykström said, he did understand the gestures. He got up, dripping with water, and put his hands in the air. In both of them there were plastic bags full of berries. His chest was red.

I died. I would have liked to live.

The red was from the lingonberries.

'What man?!' Pykström shouted in English. Then, in a mixture of English and Russian, 'You mafia kriminal. Me finski soldat!'

Berry-picker, Vatanescu explained in his own language and in a foreign one, showing him the bags.

Everyman.

Rights.

He's lying, Pykström thought, the Sicilian is lying. Even if he was telling the truth, what could be worse than these people who pick berries on other people's land, enriching themselves at their expense? Why the hell was it necessary to have a permit in order to dig a well, build a sewer or an annexe, but not to pick berries? Certainly no Sicilian had the right to pick those berries, though Harri Pykström had no intention of ever picking them himself. Even the kids from those Helsinki families made him nervous, getting lost on holiday weekends and filling their plastic cups with berries to make homemade pies.

Pykström and Vatanescu stood face to face. One was starting to feel cold because he was naked, the other because he was wet. But Pykström refused to give in, and Vatanescu did not dare to do or say anything.

The situation was resolved by Mrs Pykström, who ran down the slope and jumped on her husband's back. It was like a scene from a pantomime, or Laurel and

Hardy with two Hardies. One of whom had a serious heart defect, and so was soon out of the running. Mrs Pykström managed to slacken her husband's grip on his rifle, and it fell to the ground.

Harri Pykström sagged and collapsed on the stony bank. Vatanescu grabbed the weapon and threw it far into the brook.

Power belongs to the man who is strong.
Berries to the man with the rifle.

What was the likelihood that this trio would ever meet? Harri Pykström, born in Kirkkonummi, 1954, Mrs Pykström, born in Tapanila, Helsinki, 1958, and Vatanescu, supposedly born in three different places and three different years? Yet here they all sat now, out of breath beside a babbling brook. One scared, one craving his light beer and chaser, and one furious with her husband because of his baffling ability to bring about crises involving his heart or Sicilian berry-pickers.

Mrs Pykström asked Vatanescu who he was.

Who I am?

He took off the wet trousers, wrung them out and offered to make his grandmother Klara's berry pie as a token of good will.

'What's he saying?' Pykström asked his wife, who translated.

Pykström dragged himself upright and told Vatanescu to be on his way, either back to where he had come from, or where he was going. He was perfectly able to sort out a Sicilian, even without a rifle. He took a step towards Vatanescu, raised his arm and tried to seize him by the throat.

The rabbit jumped up on the rock it had hidden behind.

And in an instant the bad gave way to the good.

Aman who does what Vatanen did in the book and the film, Pykström kept saying. Takes to the forest, finds the true life. Forgets the conventionalities, the customs and the rules. Does what is necessary, demonstrates his civilised nature by going beyond civilisation. Pykström poured out his disillusionment with life to Vatanescu: what difference was there between town and country when you could have underfloor heating and a satellite dish in either? Harri Pykström's life would be the same wherever he was. There was no escaping destiny, no matter how much you tried.

I didn't know that an easy life is a hard life.

Vatanescu sat on the leather sofa that was moulded in the shape of Harri Pykström's backside, a can of light beer in his hand.

'You're a good man, Sicilian.'

Pykström rummaged in his video collection and, with boyish glee, shouted hurrah.

'Grrr-eat!' Mrs Pykström heard from the baby monitor on the table in the video room on the floor above, which enabled her to hear the two men talking and provide a simultaneous translation of what they were saying. The monitor had been used as an intercom ever since Harri Pykström's heart attack, so he could be in permanent voice contact with the rest of the house. Now he told his wife to translate the statement that Antti Litja's performance in the film version of *The Year of the Hare* was the finest achievement in the history of Finnish cinema. The way in which he expressed a constant state of annoyance, irritation and dissatisfaction, a kind of cumulative inward pressure. Yet at the same time a warmth of feeling towards the hare. This man did not complain, didn't pour out his feelings, but set about doing what was demanded of him.

'That's what's so wonderful about Vatanen, and that's what's so wonderful about you!'

The film's music had a melancholy beauty, and to his astonishment Vatanescu realised that he knew this story.

I know where the bridge engineers and millers in my dream came from.

Books.

I found the first one in a rubbish bin in Bucharest railway station when I was looking for food.

Vatanescu had sat down on the spot and read the book from cover to cover, forgetting about food.

This country is in it. It's not really this country; nothing here is the same as it is in those books, but this is the country that Paasilinna wrote about.

'Sicilian, you're doing exactly what Vatanen did. Telling them all to go to blazes.'

Vatanen had choices. Do you think, naked fat man, that I came to this house, to this sofa of my own free will? You tried to kill me.

Pykström described his own aspirations and said he was a man who had been emasculated. An incomplete man, wounded in the worst place, the heart. He had to live in civilisation, whether he wanted to or not, and what was worst of all, he did want to, because he wanted to live, quite simply. Not many people were willing to put their whole existence at stake.

I wish I had a quad bike, underfloor heating and a baby monitor like Pykström. I wish I had a smiling wife with a kind heart who exercised. I don't ask much, but I won't get anything. I'd be content with the football boots.

Pykström said that by setting out on his own journey Vatanescu had fulfilled a dream that thousands of other men had. They would be witnessing someone doing what they would not be able to do.

'You want the most primitive way of life, in which thoughts no longer matter and one concentrates solely on survival.'

I didn't want to go anywhere; I've just ended up all over the place. I'd willingly change places with you. I'm picking berries in a country I don't know: think about that. It's not any kind of statement. It's my life. I'm being hunted by international crime and the Finnish police.

'And now, Sicilian and hare, we are going to the sauna.'

Beggar and rabbit.

'Rabbits belong in little girls' bedrooms, in cages. If that's a rabbit, I'm a vegetarian!'

It's a rabbit.

'The Sicilian really is a stubborn fellow. But we won't quarrel about it. Let's compromise.'

Beggar and…

'…hare.'

And they agreed on this version, for the person with the power also has the power to define the one who lacks the power. Either that, or it was simply Pykström's characteristic way of expressing himself, in drunken chatter.

Meanwhile, the rabbit jumped up on Mrs Pykström's lap to watch a game show on TV, and the men went off to the sauna.

Pykström got three tubs of water ready and poured a can of beer on the stones in the sauna heater. The heat spread with the smell of grain, forcing its way into Vatanescu's lungs and under his skin. He bowed his head and held his breath. Pykström produced a whip made of twigs and told Vatanescu to turn his back to him.

Don't hit me. You're crazy. No one hits me.

'It's a form of massage,' Pykström said in Finnglish: 'Finnis masaas spesiali foor juu. From mii, Pysrömi.'

The curtains open with a remote control, but the massage is done by whipping. Who is the modern man, who the barbarian?

When Vatanescu was thoroughly red all over, Pykström asked him to do the same to him.

I won't do it.

Not to anyone.

Not even out of revenge.

Pykström leaned forward, sticking out his buttocks, and signalled with his finger that he wanted it all the way down to his toes, not forgetting his posterior. He explained that in Finland it was perfectly legal and respectable, that the men whipped their women with bunches of twigs and the women whipped their men. It was a kind of service that one needed in order to be able to resume one's endless workload the following morning.

If I perform this service, what service will I receive in exchange?

'Anything you want. Vot juu niid?'

Football boots.

Vatanescu picked up the sauna whisk with a mixture of tiredness, disappointment and bitterness. And even a slight sense of being pissed off – which made it easier for him to strike Harri Pykström as the tennis heroes of his childhood had struck the ball: forehand, backhand, forehand, backhand, forehand, smash, drop shot, forehand, forehand, passing shot to the sideline, hard cannonball.

'Thenk juu, Sicilian!' Harri Pykström shouted before running out to the ice-cold brook.

Vatanescu watched him through the steamed-up window. In the moonlight he looked like a beached walrus.

And then our hero also walked out into the cold air, lowered himself on his back into the icy current, put his head under the water and laughed, there under the world, there under the stars, beside a big baby; in the cradle of the Lapland fells Vatanescu laughed at everything and nothing.

Did the woman who gave birth to me know that at some stage in his life her only son would share a bottle of hooch with Harri Pykström? Freezing his balls off in the Arctic Circle?

'Up you get,' Pykström said, pulling Vatanescu out of the water, just as the latter had begun to feel an improvement. 'My pals don't drown.'

From the baby monitor came snoring. The men's interpreter had fallen asleep.

Pykström sat down on the wooden bench in the sauna porch, and nodded to Vatanescu to sit beside him. He opened two cans of beer and lit his cigarette with a yellow Colt lighter. Vatanescu tried to adopt the same straightforward approach to the nudity, to the heat of the sauna room, to the coldness of the air outside and the brightness of the starry sky, but could not manage it.

You can't learn this.

It's something you have to grow up with.

Vatanescu interpreted Pykström to Pykström, but in his own language.

You people are remote, and yet you get to the heart of things.

You are completely mad, but you're masters of water isolation.

'Yes, yes, Sicilian. Let's have a little sing-song.'

To judge by the rhythm, Pykström's songs were military marches. Vatanescu preferred cheerful accordion music that bounced in all directions, and love songs performed by pulsating women, but he who pays for the light beers calls the tune.

'"Finland's poor are rising..." Come on, Sicilian, sing, damn you "...broken chains despising, their suffering's cup now overflows, onward goes their army..."'

Vatanescu hummed along, but one cannot really do that to a tune one does not know. It doesn't catch – it comes from outside, not from within. Pykström went and fetched another beer from the changing room and opened it. He patted Vatanescu on the back.

'You're a good man and so is your hare. Damn it, a real bucko. The old league. The real thing. A noble comrade. Bloody hell! A berry-picker! Out to get football boots! Bloody h-e-e-e-e-lll!'

One gulp the size of the can, and then for a moment or two his foot tapped out the rhythm on the floorboards of the porch.

'"Our blows are deep, our anger will prevail, no mercy or motherland have we..." No, wait. My great-uncle was interned in the prison camp at Hennala during the Civil War, so I know how that goes, too...'

Pykström smacked his lips as he tried to remember the words. Vatanescu felt his skin: was he now so cold that he was hot? In this country his body was never at the right temperature. Everyone had to go from a sauna at a hundred degrees Celsius to water at freezing point, children and old folk included!

'"Arise, ye workers from your slumbers..."'

Vatanescu knew this one.

'"... arise, ye citizens of want..."'

At school, in neat rows, they all had to sing and they

all did. The words didn't matter at all, because it was all about feeling. Music pierces the armour, it penetrates deeper than reason.

"'And the last fight let us face!'"

The echo spread through the sauna in two languages, and through the universe, too. It spread up the hill, in through the triple-glazed windows of Harri Pykström's pine log villa to the windowsill where the rabbit was asleep.

"'The Interna-a-a-a-t-iona-a-a-al-e uni-i-i-i-i-tes the hu-u-u-uman race!'"

Yegor Kugar's life was starting to go downhill. The number of contracts he got began to dwindle, because his rights to extortion and torture had been removed. Then he was told he would have to pay rent for the place he was living in. Yegor Kugar's mental balance was affected, and that was quite new to him.

'I admit it. My head just couldn't take it. My nerves have been in a mess ever since I got my ear cut off in St Petersburg, but do I look like the kind of guy who would go to the mental health centre? When you blow a gasket, the engine goes haywire. The moped does a hundred and twenty miles an hour and I'm standing upright on the saddle with a bandage over my eyes. I had dreams about Vatanescu in which I killed him. By drowning him, strangling him, smothering him with a pillow, watching him pass away. After that I had some really moronic dreams where Vatanescu and I were out fishing together or playing tennis in polo shirts and giving each other high fives. In the morning I'd wake soaked in sweat beside whatever broad I was with, and it would be quite a few minutes before I could get it up again.'

That is indeed how it is sometimes, and all of us who have ever worked know the theory of shit. The steak flambé that is eaten on the top storey may end up pouring down as diarrhoea on the employees on the floors below. For that reason, or perhaps because of his misanthropy and anthropophobia, Yegor Kugar now covered his eyes with large sunglasses even when the sky was overcast; he now wore a cap, and a hood on top of it. The logo on the cap said The Bear, and yesterday's truth had now become a post-modern irony, or rather, a cruel game.

'The guys from the *krysha*, the international protection racket, asked me what was up in the Grand Duchy. Who's responsible? The accounts are drying up, the tramps are charging deductions and daily expenses. Hello? Every zero day is ten grand lost and I would have to find that dough somewhere.

'I'm responsible. I come up with the explanations.

'Except I didn't have one. For example, how was it that Balthazar, who had been earning several hundred euros a week, now made no more than two euros a month? Well, perhaps the real fucking reason was that he'd last been seen playing the accordion in Örnsköldsvik, Sweden.'

Chapter Seven

*In which we find Eldorado, Goodluck Jeffersson and Urmas
Õunap, and in which Vatanescu appears to Yegor*

Vatanescu awoke to the smell of herbs, tomato, feta
cheese, smoked ham and onion. His gaze travelled
along the ceiling and the walls.

Did I die?

But few are the graves that come with a television
screen on which a bearded Finnish runner has just
won an Olympic gold medal, in spite of a fall, while
Anssi Kukkonen commentates by shouting in the background. Vatanescu turned his head and saw a naked
Harri Pykström dozing in an armchair with his feet on
a footstool, the remote control in his right hand.

Vatanescu got up, put his blanket over his host and
removed the extinguished cigarette from between his
fingers, then, blinking, returned upstairs to the ground
floor.

The rabbit was nibbling grated carrot on the kitchen
table. Mrs Pykström said good morning and invited
Vatanescu to try her Mediterranean omelette.

Vatanescu drank a glass of water. Then a second, and
a third. A hangover in a strange house is an existen-
tial crisis, because instead of concrete beneath one's feet
one has a shifting marsh. One doesn't know who one is,
what one remembers, what one ought to remember. Mrs
Pykström said that when Vatanescu had finished eating
it would be time for him to leave.

Sorry, did I do something wrong?

'Harri will be in no state to drive until this evening. I've got some buckets ready. In the cold pack there are berries, salad and a carton of goat's milk for the rabbit.'

Vatanescu changed into an arctic snowsuit that was several sizes too large for him. By tightening the cords and rolling up the sleeves and trouser bottoms he managed to make it fit. Mrs Pykström gave the rabbit a pair of bootees and a baby bonnet that had belonged to her children.

On the van's radio the announcer was listing the temperatures for the coast and archipelago from the various weather stations. The rabbit lay in an empty bucket on Vatanescu's lap, and Vatanescu gazed at the red and brown tints of the forests, he gazed ahead at the gently rising contours of the landscape, he gazed at the stretches of water and lines of fells that glittered in the distance. Between the dwarf birches a man or a reindeer would trot into view for a moment. Unexpected words suddenly issued from Mrs Pykström's mouth.

'Harri has some boyish dreams. Harri is an old man who is dying. How can I make him see that?'

Yes.

'He'll listen to you, but not to anyone else. He's never listened to what anyone else says.'

I didn't say anything to him. I don't know him. You mustn't mix me up in anything.

'That's just it. You didn't say anything to Harri.'

I want to go home. I want a home.

I want football boots for my son.

'Do you think I'm really interested in Zumba? Under normal conditions I'd be studying the cultural significance of that craze, but here I have to be a part of it.'

Mrs Pykström turned the van off the main road and onto a forest track. She got out to move the Forestry

Commission barrier aside and drove deep into the forest.

Mrs Pykström unloaded the buckets from the back of the van and pointed in the direction of where Vatanescu would find the yellow berries. She rummaged in the pockets of her windcheater, found a mobile phone and gave it to him. There was a pre-paid SIM card in it, with one phone number in its memory. Harri Pykström's number, which he was to call as soon as he had found the berries. They would come and collect him.

The trees creaked as if they were talking to one another. While Vatanescu studied the map, the rabbit caught sight of a lemming. The creatures looked at each other, perhaps wondering what fellow member of their species had arrived, or what rival was trying to usurp their territory. Vatanescu chased away the last effects of his hangover with a handful of pungent lingonberries. Mrs Pykström had marked the best places for berries with a red circle, the slightly less good areas with a blue one, and on the least important areas she had put a cross.

Bilberries.

Lingonberries.

Bilberries. Lingonberries. Bilberries lingonberries bilberries lingonberries.

The rabbit grew tired, came to sit at Vatanescu's feet, and from there returned to the sling.

Let's look until we find something.

According to the map we're only a mile or two from our destination.

Now and then Vatanescu lost his bearings, now and then the compass needle whirled unsteadily and several times he felt like giving up. But he trusted in what his fat Finnish friend and his wife had told him, and so he decided to make one last search. If he didn't find anything he would have to look in the mirror and admit his own failure. He would have to go home empty-handed, blisters on his heels, his spirits shattered.

Exactly on the edge of the circle that Mrs Pykström had drawn he saw the first glimmer of gold.

From tussock to tussock, with duckboards in between, then churning knee-deep through marshes, the beggar and the hare went on side by side.

Eldorado.

Football boots.

Cloudberries.

Vatanescu pulled himself through the marsh like some legendary Finnish skiing champion of former days.

Come to daddy.

No sacrifice will have been in vain.

After a scree, a hillock and another scree, before their eyes stretched a marsh the size of four football pitches, bordered by hills and bursting with orange-yellow berries just waiting to be picked.

I'm... rich...

Served on Lapland cheese, as the base for a liqueur, made into jam, as a flavouring – the further the process of refinement was taken, the greater the profit. Vatanescu thrust both of his hands into the berries and dug, showering a handful all over himself. He chewed them, soft as raspberry on the outside, on the inside a grainy sensation, the seeds.

Sour.

Unpleasant.
Never mind.
They're scarce.
So they're expensive.

His mood brightening, Vatanescu began to fill the buckets.

I'll be the owner of the team my son plays for. He'll have the best football boots that money can buy, I'll teach him how to tie double knots and I'll stand at the edge of the pitch.

I won't shout like a madman. I won't yell abuse at the other team. I won't need to.

Miklos will be the best. The son of a newly rich berry-picker.

Vatanescu picked berries late into the evening and on into early morning, without missing a single one, and when dawn broke he had filled all of the Pykströms' buckets. He made the tent that Mrs Pykström had given him into a large bag some five feet wide, and soon it too was full. Leaving the now denuded marsh behind him, Vatanescu lugged the tent back to his base camp, put it beside the buckets and felt his pockets.

Harri Pykström will take me and the berries to a place where I can sell them.

The phone?
The phone!

On the way Vatanescu's phone had fallen into the depths of the marsh, where it mouldered away and oxidised. If anyone ever found it again it would probably be an archaeologist who was studying the toils and troubles of humanity in the first decade of the twenty-first century, in the age of accumulation.

Don't panic.

Vatanescu looked at his compass. He would easily find the direction from which he had come.

Two steps forward, one step back.

A road.
A car and a road.
A main road. That way.
I can carry eight buckets at once.

Vatanescu found a long, strong tree branch to make a carrying device. He lifted the branch onto his shoulders like the slaves in Egypt and the women in Häme. He asked the rabbit to go on ahead, to lead the way, to help them avoid getting wet.

Where there's a road, there's a man. Someone will surely come. A rescuer. A German camping trailer. A local lad in his drag car.

After the third heavy step there was an explosion.
Gravel, stones and moss flew above him.

Now I died.

Vatanescu had lost his hearing. He could hear nothing outside his body, but the beating of his heart thumped inside his head as if the neighbours were playing Rammstein on their stereo.

I didn't die?
Did the rabbit die?

The rabbit sat trembling on a lump of stone that had fallen beside it. Vatanescu approached the rabbit very quietly, took it in his cupped hands and hid it in the shelter of his armpit. Then he gathered the remaining buckets of berries.

A military exercise?
A war?
A nuclear explosion?
The end of the world?

Vatanescu set off through the marsh in a random

112

direction, guided now not by the compass or by reason but by the fear of death and the state of panic from which he was only a moment away. Suddenly under his feet the ground was firmer, more even, a path trodden by people or reindeer.

If there's a path…

…at its end there'll be a road…

If there's a road…

…at its end there'll be…

…a human being.

The path continued towards some dwarf birches and on to somewhere beyond his field of vision.

For an explosion you need a human being. The author of the explosion will have a car. The car will have a tow bar. It can be used to attach a trailer. The berries will go in the trailer.

Vatanescu felt his body shake, and wondered whether it was simply the beating of his heart. Probably not, as the shaking seemed to begin in the soles of his feet.

It was an accelerating rhythm, tuh-toom, muh-toom, buh-boom!

Perhaps I really did die.

Perhaps I'm in hell.

The decision to build the largest shopping mall, hotel complex, entertainment and golf centre in the Nordic countries had been easy to make by drawing a circle on the map with a pair of compasses. A radius of a hundred and ninety miles with a customer catchment area that included four countries. In addition, a retirement home with an exotic view. The decision made, the construction company began to receive reservations from the United States, Canada and dictators in Central America. In the municipality of Raattama, an ice rink where the

Finnish ice hockey team would play in the intercontinental championships. Clothes shops, car dealerships, supermarkets, an equipment rental company.

Commercial activity would give birth to a town.

The town would need public services, healthcare, a library, schools. Its construction would be partially financed by public funding.

It would be like a modern Helsinki–Stockholm car ferry combined with the building sites of Kostomuksha and the gold-mining towns of Russian Karelia. It would be a new Las Vegas, as the developers Taive Sikari and Kerkko Kolmonen had said in their inaugural speeches. Then the ribbon had been cut, the foundation stone laid, and smiles provided for the photographers.

With the contract signed, a workforce was needed for the construction project. Kolmonen and Sikari did not intend to conform to Finnish legislation on wage levels and working hours, never mind the demands of the trade unions and their shop stewards. Workers from other parts of the world – slaves, migrants or indigenous peoples – have always built mankind's most remarkable edifices. Finns, American Indians, Chinese. The workforce would not be exploited, but the pay would be based on the men's initial pay grade and status in their home country. Six euros would not get an unemployed Finn off the sofa except to go and buy his lottery ticket. An Estonian would leave his family, live in a caravan and work fourteen hours a day.

The work on the project was now nearly halfway complete. Trucks drove in and out of the gates, cranes blocked the sky as they moved the prefabricated units into place.

Vatanescu crawled out of the bushes onto the muddy main road. In front of him towered a large sign: NSDAC IS BUILDING THE NATIONAL IDEA PARK ON THE SITE OF THE NATIONAL PARK. PROJECT COMPLETION IS SCHEDULED FOR SPRING 2013.

Vatanescu shook the mud from his clothes and made sure that the rabbit was all right. The rabbit quivered and put its ears back.

There's no hurry.

Calm down.

Don't panic. I'm going to stop this truck.

Vatanescu walked into the middle of the road and stretched out his arms. The Scania truck braked and stopped an elbow's length away from him. The driver's name was Õunap. In his former existence he had been a petty Estonian crook – smuggling cigarettes and alcohol into Finland, running offbeat chauffeuring jobs and paying hardly any tax.

After the East European states and their peoples settled down he had fallen in love, married, reproduced and vowed to support his family by honest means. There were enough building sites in Finland to keep him in work until the year 2000 and even a little beyond. Õunap saved enough capital to start his own business back home.

In Estonia Õunap's company, Sheet Metal and Concrete, prospered at first. Soon it all went belly-up. Economic fluctuations + the international financial crisis = bankruptcy of Sheet Metal and Concrete. He had to return to Finland and take the first low-paid job he could find. Which was better by half than the crumpled banknotes of his homeland.

Now Õunap seethed in the cabin of his truck, hammered on the window and sounded the horn. He wound the window down and swore in all the languages he knew. Vatanescu's hearing was still non-existent.

Let's get my berries. I'll give you thirty per cent.

The driver leaned his torso out of the window of the truck, grabbed Vatanescu by the ears and shook him. Out of his ears fell gravel, moss and little stones. As his hearing returned, a soundscape of the end of the world – that post-modernist radio feature – invaded Vatanescu's consciousness.

Forty per cent?

The driver opened the door on the passenger side and told Vatanescu to get in. He had to combine four badly spoken languages in order to obtain some kind of comprehension. Õunap demanded to know why the man wasn't at Kittilä Airport at the right time. He had wasted three hours for nothing, and without pay. Was the man stupid or just slow? Why was it only dickheads that came from Poland?

I'm not from Poland.

I'm Vatanescu.

I have berries.

You can have forty-five per cent.

Õunap told him to forget the berries and listen. All that mattered was laying the concrete for the multi-storey car park's D wing. The work could not go forward because the pump was in the back of the truck that Õunap was driving. At his feet the Pole would find a helmet, a reflective jacket, steel-tipped boots and a tool belt.

I'm not a concrete-layer. I'm an everyman.

I'm a berry-picker. I really am.

'Stick your berries up your arse. You're a concrete layer. A nozzleman.'

In protective boots and helmet, cement gun in hand, in a group of three. The team was made up of Vatanescu and Õunap and the third member, Goodluck Jeffersson, a Ghanaian-Norwegian giant who had arrived at the National Idea Park site after working on oilrigs and fish processing plants. In Ghana he had earned a doctorate, but the role of committed and cool intellectual had evaporated on a boat where Goodluck Jeffersson and 2,456 other subsistence-challenged people had crossed the Mediterranean and reached Italy.

Vatanescu stuck it for one day and then for another, and then halfway through that second day for the first time he remembered the berries. As he moved around, the rabbit sat inside his work overall, and from time to time it peeped out of the collar to see if anything had changed, if it would dare to leave, but nonetheless preferred to remain in the thoroughly reassuring smell of Vatanescu's sweat. One by one, all Vatanescu's thoughts and feelings vanished from his consciousness, and all that remained was the cement gun, of which he was now a part.

After the third day a forty-eight-hour break began.

Jeffersson and Õunap carried Vatanescu by his arms and legs to an abandoned shack which the men had taken over to live in, fed up with their caravan existence. In the shack it was always either too cold or too hot, and mice ran about on the floor and in the food cupboards, and they were even joined by a rat.

Jeffersson had installed electricity in the shack's twelve square yards, and there was a fire in the wood stove. It was as homely as two heterosexual males living together could make it. On the walls there were photos of the men's children and of the person who Jeffersson claimed was the world's most beautiful woman, the javelin thrower Trine Hattestad, who he thought was both warm and easy-going. Jeffersson thought he could spend the rest of his life with a woman like her with relatively little conflict, in contrast to his experiences with his previous four women.

Vatanescu was already asleep when the men carried him in, and on an upper bunk he subsided into an even deeper slumber. Shyly the rabbit emerged from the overall. It jumped straight into Õunap's lap.

Õunap was stirring a big saucepan of soup. Vatanescu asked how long he had slept.

'Eighteen hours.'

The microwave beeped and Õunap took out a vegetarian pizza for the rabbit. He remarked that the rabbit had really cheered the place up; it was almost as though they had female company. Nothing to do with copulation of course, but something to keep them on their toes, for male farting and blathering became tedious after a while. Since the rabbit's arrival they had had to pay more attention to where they threw their dirty socks and empty beercans.

Vatanescu tried to turn round, but every muscle and tendon in his body hurt. Õunap noticed his groans of pain and said that his muscles would eventually realise that it was no good complaining, as the work never stopped, not ever.

Vatanescu forced himself onto his stomach and pulled himself to the edge of the bunk. He observed the log walls, the greasy window and Jeffersson fiddling with the joystick of a Playstation.

The berries. Let's distribute them. Thirty-three, thirty-three, thirty-three.

Õunap stopped stirring the saucepan with his

screwdriver and poured Vatanescu a large bowlful of steaming reindeer tail soup. When Vatanescu had swallowed a dozen spoonfuls and was properly awake, Õunap asked him to listen.

'Berry-picking is on the way out. Like reindeer herding.'

Õunap said that in the modern world you needed to be a capital investor, not a berry-picker. You had to be a retailer or an entertainment provider. You had to establish a trade name, preferably a general partnership or a limited company, so you would pay less tax.

'Dividends, expenses allowances and that sort of thing,' Goodluck Jeffersson chimed in, without raising his head from his 110-metre hurdle race.

'Look out of the window,' Õunap said.

Nothing was visible through the grease and the passage of decades, but Õunap asked him to imagine.

'That used to be the Pallas Fells. Tomorrow there will be a hotel there. The old hills have been put out to grass; they're going to make a giant slope out of them. Ski-lifts, a ski-jump, a downhill ski-slope.'

Listen! Really... there are masses... of yellow berries... They're safe there, I've hidden them.

'Vatanescu,' Õunap said, looking him in the eye.

Well?

'That cloudberry marsh.'

Yes?

'They've made it into a car park.'

Water mingled with cement. The concrete bubbled. There were so many glass structures that the finished building would look unfinished. The floors, the walls and ceilings would be put in place, and there they would stay for another two decades until the building was demolished to make way for something new. Cables, sewers, joist frames, panel walls, tiling, drains, a backup generator, security systems.

One small piece of a larger whole, surrounded by machines, people and explosive substances, our hero resigned himself to his fate, which was better than it looked at first sight. Piece by piece a new world was being born – a world of shopping – and being a part of its construction felt satisfying to Vatanescu. Each working day had a meaning. In one corner Jeffersson had made a miniature shack for the rabbit, and the three men lived in their home like brothers, or pupils at a school for boys.

Vatanescu pumped concrete, carried joists, learned the skills of carpentry from Jeffersson, was soon handy with the spirit level and the keyhole saw, mastered the mitre box and the laminate cutter. From Õunap he learned how to spend the evenings productively, too: playing poker with the few Finns who were present on the site. On payday he could sometimes increase his wages fivefold.

Six hundred… seven hundred… seven hundred and forty euros.

We're getting there.

Õunap took Vatanescu to Muonio in his truck. At a grocer's they bought cigarette papers, tinned tuna, cut-price meat that was near its sell-by date, a large pack of Finnish light beer in a suitcase-shaped cardboard box and three liver sausages, Jeffersson's favourite snack.

Then to the sports shop.

I'm familiar with Adidas, Nike and Reebok. Is there a brand that's even better? Money is no object.

It was the wrong time of year, the wrong season, the sales clerk said. Now they were waiting for the start of

the winter and the stockrooms were bursting with tradi-
tional skis, cross-country skis, downhill skis. Did they
want those? Or maybe fishing tackle or hunting gloves?
Snowshoes? Football boots would not be coming in
until next April, as football was not the favourite leisure
pastime of young people in Lapland.

'They're more into motor sledging, skiing, fishing,
you know. Wilderness sports.'

Jeffersson patted Vatanescu on the shoulder and told
him not to lose heart. They could order the boots over
the Internet on Jeffersson's laptop.

From the infinite selection they clicked on the boots
advertised by the world's most highly paid footballer.
This gel-haired twenty-something street urchin was
paid tens of thousands for every minute he lived and
breathed and fumed. The price of one of Vatanescu's,
Õunap's and Jeffersson's minutes was about a million
times lower.

Vatanescu's order was made; now all he had to do
was enter his Internet banking details.

Bank code? Credit card number? Address? Name?
Right.
I'm off to bed.

Vatanescu's anger made him pour his concrete so
well that he was promoted to the rank of truck driver.
Now the Romanian beggar who had no driver's licence
took his turn in fetching new arrivals from the airport
and the train station. No one knew who he was, few
were interested in someone else's past, and the future
was the same for them all: hopefully better. He was
called Ivan the Bulgarian Bar Bender or Miroslaw the
Pole, Son of Bronislaw or the Albanian Fox.

Yegor Kugar had had to make certain adjustments to his choices for copulation. The sudden and surprising reduction in his market value was showing in the quality of his partners. In his previous life he had been able to pick up anyone at all, and that anyone had come running. He attached the bait, cast the line in the water and always got a bite. But now the value of his stock was in free fall.

'I had to take what I could get, and it was surplus crap. Outside the social security office in Tikkurila I found an ugly bitch from Koivukylä and held onto her, because Yegor doesn't sleep alone. Disgusting tits like potholders and a butt like a beanbag, cellulite as thick as the palm of your hand. But she was warm and she was a woman.

'The lady from Koivukylä was of the opinion that as Yegor had such a nice car it was best not to upset him; she was prepared to take the rough with the smooth as long as my 7 Series BMW with rear propulsion purred under her flabby ass. It had an electric roof window, roof-mounted DVD, refrigerator, turbos, the lot. All you could wish for, in cash, just name your currency.'

But Yegor Kugar's employer took his company car away. One morning instead of the BMW there was a 1985 Lada Niva with cardboard and duct tape in one of its side windows and hardly a drop of petrol in the tank. The car was exactly the same model that Yegor's mother had queued for in the land of the Soviets but never got. A message was pinned to the steering wheel with a knife, advising Yegor to keep a sense of proportion. He ought to count himself lucky he still had a car at all. Yegor walked to the nearest service station and with a crumpled five-euro note bought some 98 octane in empty lemonade bottles.

'No one else offered to employ me. I called all the numbers that used to say cheerily that they had a job here, a job there, go and collect plasma TVs from Kerava and sell them on in Malmi. Pick up three Czech broads and put them on sale for a week in the flat in Kamppi.

'At first I got angry replies. Then I got no replies at all.

'Nice, to be blackballed. Thanks, Vatanescu.

'A fucking awful winter set in, one that froze balls and cars and trains. I ordered Kamagra off the Web, the poor man's Viagra, so I could screw again and at least have something in my life that worked. I downed all the pills at once and a moment later got an erection like a red-hot poker. I asked the broad to forget about getting dressed that day. But she had other ideas.

'She confided that she found it humiliating to sit in the front of an unheated Lada. She couldn't have warm feelings for the owner of a cold Lada. She explained that she'd be happy to go out with a *rich* Russian, but there were plenty of poor Finns at home too.

'Fuck, it's hard to listen to that kind of thing when your cock is XL size. The broad started talking about how her parents had a Lada when she was a little girl, something about traumas and class conflicts. They'd taken her to Mänttä every summer with the radio playing Sinikka Sokka and those bearded guys from Agitprop. It didn't mean anything to me; all I know is that a *sokka* is a pin you get in hand grenades.'

123

And Yegor Kugar was left sitting naked on a kitchen stool, with a futile erection in his groin. His girlfriend, his other half, his lady, call her what you will, Kaarina, got her things together, put them in a plastic bag and left the building. Yegor was unable to act, unable to stop her, unable to keep her by force, or even throw a beercan after her, which was his usual way of resolving conjugal crises. He rose from his stool and looked out of the window. Kaarina was getting into a car that was waiting by the front door.

'It was some ex-ice hockey player. I lost my broad to some guy named Niko from Hyvinkää.

'On my first night alone I cracked up. After that I could only sleep with the help of pills, and I took them in the daytime too. I paid a last visit to my former employees Pirita and Marketta on Vaasankatu Street, who gave me enough cash to last a week, and from the four beggars who were left I took everything they had. Then I retired to my pad.

'My body was used to screwing at least once a day. If it's any less frequent than that, my dick juice goes up to my head. I lose my concentration, my nerves go to pieces, I make the wrong decisions or I don't make any decisions at all.

'I lay on my mattress covered in sweat, trembling all over; it was the same kind of shaking and fear of death and longing for death I experienced when I came off opium in Yobistan. And the same lack of interest in my own fate.'

The only friend Yegor Kugar had left was an Indian gentleman named Naseem Hasapatilalati, who ran the convenience store downstairs. If they had anything in common, it was loneliness, melancholy, and a seething bitterness that had become the most powerful fuel of their lives.

A week after the Organisation had relieved Yegor of his duties, the landlord rang his doorbell. When Yegor failed to open up, the landlord went away and returned with the police.

'Do you think I have a clean credit history, with banking IDs and a savings account? Do you think the rental agreement was in my own name? It was in the name of Kostomuksha Pipe Systems PLC, and now the rent had not been paid. After the palace in Moscow I had only lived in places that the Organisation had arranged or dictated. Sometimes they were basements, sometimes they were luxury penthouses you got to by taking a lift from the base-ment straight to the thirty-eighth floor.

'I looked inside my leather jacket and found my last banknotes, the currency of four different coun-tries, pushed them through the door slot, and got a few weeks of peace. I phoned down to Naseem at the convenience store to bring me grub.'

One very ordinary Thursday, as Vatanescu ate grand-ma's meatballs from the microwave, the first snow began to float down from the sky. Back in his homeland it only snowed on the loftiest, sharpest mountain peaks. Here it was all over the place; the cotton wool covered everything. It settled in a smooth, even mass, and it was cold but bright. It covered the earth-moving equip-ment and the unfinished buildings, and it blotted out all human traces.

Vatanescu walked in the snow in his long johns and bare feet. Õunap slammed the door to keep the heat in, and called to the madman to come inside before he caught pneumonia. Vatanescu spread his hands and turned round. He fell on his back. He opened his mouth and tasted snowflakes on the tip of his tongue.

Life is a fairytale.

The developer Kerkko Kolmonen knocked at the door of the shack at five in the morning. He promised to double the wages of his best construction team for all the days they managed to knock off the original schedule. They knew, however, that if the weather got any colder or it started to snow in earnest, the pumping of concrete would be impossible. The cement guns would freeze.

'Five hundred euros in advance for each guy,' Kolmonen said.

Now I'm the richest man in my village.

Let's get to work.

At the same moment, seven hundred miles to the south, Iina Rautee was studying the satellite photographs of the national park site. She had found her vocation. Her job was to save the world. She must save it from machines, human beings and the all-destructive greed of capital. She regarded herself as free from the fetters of money and material goods. The world also had to be saved from the thoughtlessness of her parents. Her mother used makeup that was tested on animals. Her father ate health yoghurts manufactured by a multinational company and refused to give them up in favour of organic products.

The only poster in Iina Rautee's room was one of Ulrike Meinhof. As part of the literature course she had taken at school she had read an autofictional novel about a German terrorist group and wanted to be part of something similar, in the same way that the boys in the class dreamed of a professional career in ice hockey or rock music.

Terrorism was exciting. It took a lot more balls to be Ulrike Meinhof than it did to be Andy McCoy of Hanoi Rocks. With bombs and assault rifles towards a better world, sacrificing one's own life and those of the capitalist pigs.

Chaining oneself to a bulldozer: it was eighty per cent nature conservation, twenty per cent S&M.

Iina had left a note on the kitchen table to say that when reading week was over she would come back for the final exams, but that just as probably she would join the ranks of the revolution.

The revolution demands, the revolution sets free, she wrote, quoting the South American singer and songwriter Alfonso Padilla.

During the same two months that Õunap, Jeffersson and Vatanescu were pulling out all the stops to get the work finished, the environmental organisation Nature-Mili was preparing an expedition. As Vatanescu put his head on the pillow again after another cold day that had turned sweaty, a group from Nature-Mili set off for Lapland. They had bought their truck from a dubious, one-eared Russian in Helsinki's suburb of Kalasatama.

And one day at sunrise Vatanescu did what he always did. He washed his face in the brook, splashed his stubbly cheeks a couple of times and was ready to build a world of shopping. For company he had the reindeer, who like him were revving themselves out of their morning stiffness.

Vatanescu urinated on the snow as he whistled the song he had sung with Harri Pykström. He had just finished shaking himself dry when he suddenly stopped whistling.

In front of him stood three rows of people who were chained to the bulldozers with handcuffs and cable clamps. They began to chant in rhythm:

'Sa-ave the nation-al pa-rk!'

And then something totally baffling:

'Sa-ave Vata-nes-cu!'

Vatanescu pinched the skin of his stomach. Yes, he was awake. Iina Rautee shouted to him to stop, to come and join the group of demonstrators.

'We're here to save you!' Iina cried. 'Vii seiv ju!'

Thanks.

But no thanks.

I've been saved once already.

I demanded and believed.

I cut the emblem of the dictatorship out of my country's flag with a knife.

That should have been freedom, too.

Buzzing overhead was a helicopter, with a cameraman leaning out of it. Vatanescu raised his eyes. More helicopters were coming; it was like *Apocalypse Now*. The helicopters were from the public and private television channels.

We didn't get freedom.

We got the flesh trade.

We got vodka bars.

We got hamburger bars and investment banks.

We had to leave and go somewhere, among you – whoever you are.

Iina Rautee purred with satisfaction; the pictures would be on CNN and all over the world. Activism now! Now! And at their centre was Vatanescu, filmed by all eight cameras. One camera zoomed in on his eyes, on the depths of his brown pupils that were filled with weary bewilderment.

You don't know what you're doing.

You're spoiling everything.

Vatanescu turned round and tried to continue onwards.

Go away.

Go away, will you.

I'm shutting my ears, go away, I'm shutting my eyes, get lost. I'm leaving.

Vatanescu collided with a group of cameramen who had just landed, and a sports reporter who had been covering the skiing championships nearby. Apparently the Finns could have been among the eight best teams, but they hadn't made it. The reporter had a question ready for Vatanescu.

'How does it feel?'

Won't I ever be allowed to do anything in peace?

Vatanescu tried to move the sports reporter out of the way. When that didn't work, he stepped off the path.

This step took him straight into the arms of Iina Rautee, who pulled him towards her. Our hero was in the wrong place at the wrong time, like Charlie Chaplin when the plank a big man is carrying hits him on the back of the head, and that plank is the world.

Hands took hold of Vatanescu's arms and tried to bind them with cables; the sports reporter thrust a microphone in front of his mouth; a group of cameramen from Finnish TV arrived, then one from Sámi Radio, then another from Sixty Minutes. Even Hannu Karpo's fur hat could be glimpsed among the crowd.

I wish you would all calm down.
That would be more businesslike.

One of the demonstrators pulled a rain cape with the Nature-Mili logo over Vatanescu's overalls. On the back a slogan demanded an end to ecological violence and the assassination or at least immediate re-education of the leaders of the G8. Vatanescu tore himself free.

Rabbit!

Run!

Yegor Kugar was walking along Helsinki's Hämeentie Road, where the wind blew from six directions at once. It was eight o'clock, but Yegor had no idea if it was am or pm. Anyway, it didn't matter.

'I never complained about the climate in Penisstan, and I didn't complain in Bluesland either, but in front of Naseem's store I did. The wind stung and whipped. I would have preferred to stay under the covers with the curtains shut and my head empty. I tried to light a smoke, but the wind had other ideas. I stuck my hands in my pockets as deep as they would go – and they went right to the bottom, for there wasn't a single rouble or dollar there. I put my collar up and wondered if I looked like Robert De Niro in *Taxi Driver*.

'Hell, no, I looked like what I was, a total loser.

'I opened the door and left the wind outside. I asked for a pack of Red North State and a cup of black coffee. That's what I lived on. The red and the black. Naseem's coffee was like oil; my life was like sump oil.

'Naseem was pleased that I'd managed to poke my

nose out of doors and thought I ought to do more of that. Take my life in a new direction.'

But Yegor's life did have a direction, and it was down. What had brought him to Naseem Hasapatilalati's store was a disconnected phone line. Yegor Kugar could no longer deliver his orders as he was accustomed to. He had lost interest in everything, his morning erection had abandoned him, his evenings were without passion, at night he had no desire to go out looking for action and fooling around.

Yegor tried to find a crumb of comfort in his local newspaper, which Naseem Hasapatilalati ordered for him at his own expense. Such friendliness touched Yegor but also made him suspicious. He did not believe in altruism or disinterested motives. No one had ever done anything for him for nothing, and vice versa.

'Maybe Naseem wasn't from Calcutta at all, but Nazareth.

'I read the ice hockey results and the match report for Avangard Omsk – things weren't going too well for that team, and the start of the season determines what will happen later on. It was like what happened to me after Vatanescu's pig-feast. Now the team had gone and recruited a Finnish coach plus some third-line eager beavers from Hämeenlinna and Lahti, and that didn't look good.

'I lit a cigarette. Naseem said that smoking wasn't allowed indoors, but he always said that. It was our private joke, because in St Petersburg and Calcutta you can set fire to accounts, and to people, any time you want; the officials from the EU are hardly likely to come and bother you with their directives.

'I had a fit of coughing, hawked up some red

muck on the floor, wheezing, rattling; I didn't know if it was blood or morning phlegm. In some ways I couldn't have cared if it was lung cancer and the last days of Kugar.'

The doorbell in the entrance rang, and the evening newspapers were brought into the store. Naseem cut the ties on the bundles and lifted the papers onto the counter. He took the placard and fitted it into the holder.

Yegor had moved on from the sports pages to the comics, which failed to make him laugh. He found it especially irritating that there were people in the world who were able to draw pictures as their job, who got respect for it, even fame in some cases. Yegor thought bitterly of the two whole decades he had sacrificed to the Organisation, without a pension or healthcare benefits. Always available, taking all the risks of a small businessman, and all the thanks he got had been the boot.

Yegor crushed his cigarette beneath his shoe and finished his coffee. In the bottom of the cardboard cup there was a black residue that resembled what was left of Yegor's vitality and powers. What had once been strong, steaming coffee, now reduced to a crumpled cup that missed the rubbish bin when you threw it.

Yegor looked out of the window. The short walk back to his front door seemed like miles. He said goodbye to Naseem and stepped outside. Sleet was falling. A bus was skidding at the bus stop; some alcoholics were singing a march tune.

Yegor thought what he had known ever since he was a child. That human beings were animals. Both physically and metaphorically. All without exception, us, you and them.

Naseem Hasapatilalati carried his placard holder out to the street.

Yegor Kugar glanced at the placard, though he didn't understand what it said.

He didn't need to, as the picture spoke for itself.

'My legs gave way under me. That idiot Vatanescu was looking me in the eye.'

VATANESCU FROM ROMANIA WORKS FOR LESS THAN THE MINIMUM WAGE AND LIVES IN INHUMAN CONDITIONS. ARE THE LARGE COMPANIES NEGLECTING MAN AND THE ENVIRONMENT, IS THIS THE PRICE OF GLOBALISATION?

Evening Gazette

ALL CONSTRUCTION WORK ON THE NATIONAL PARK SITE HAS BEEN HALTED UNTIL ISSUES RELATING TO LEGISLATION, NATURE CONSERVATION AND WORKING CONDITIONS HAVE BEEN RESOLVED.

Evening Gazette

A RARE SPECIES OF RABBIT HAS BEEN SPOTTED IN THE AREA.

Evening Gazette

SUSPECTED IRREGULARITIES IN FINANCING OF NATIONAL IDEA PARK. LABOURERS' PAY CLAIMED AS MILEAGE ALLOWANCES, DAILY EXPENSES AND EQUIPMENT HIRE.

Evening Gazette

KERKKO KOLMONEN MISSING. LAST SEEN IN PATTAYA.

Evening Gazette

Chapter Eight

In which Vatanescu becomes a magician's assistant and lover, and in which Yegor is himself again

'Sorry lads,' said the only developer's representative who had dared to remain on the site. He had been obliged to sack Vatanescu, Urmas Õunap, Goodluck Jeffersson and eighty-seven other construction workers – Poles, Russians, Finns and Ghanaians – without pay.

The coffers were empty. All further work was banned. The project would be frozen for decades, and environmental organisations were breathing down its neck. The only possible future activity would be the restoration of the devastated fells.

'We'll call you,' the developer's representative said. 'There's no point in you calling us.'

Three thousand euros in unpaid back wages.

'Do I look as though I have any money on me?'

I'm three thousand euros short.

I'm short of a pair of football boots.

'Did we have a contract? Not as far as I recall. If there was, you can claim what's owed to you from wage security.'

With this the man tried to flee, but ran straight into the arms of the police, who handcuffed him and asked him politely to get into the back of a Ford Mondeo. The guardians of the law promised to come back and fetch the rest of the gang when the ringleaders were all in custody. Work permits and identity documents would be checked, and those workmen whose papers were not in order would get a nice warm cell.

Better get moving.

Follow your own path, wherever it takes you.

To the end.

Vatanescu ran with Jeffersson and Õunap to the shack. Then, with the rabbit under his arm, and his belongings flung into an overnight bag, he set off with them on the trek out of the National Park.

After they had trudged five or six miles through the snow they stopped at a shelter to eat. With his strong, gleaming white teeth Goodluck Jeffersson tore open a pack of sausages. Õunap manufactured some barbecue sticks with a carpet knife and Vatanescu made a fire. In the course of these months in the National Idea Park he had learned the right way to handle bark, woodchips and twigs, knew how to determine the wind's direction with his finger, and how to save matches.

There was silence, the firelight glimmered on the men's faces, the sausage skins popped, fat hissed on the embers. On the sausages the men spread mustard from a yellow tube. They had acquired a taste for it during their work on the site. The rabbit passed from lap to lap. They all took turns at giving it a scratch, and thanks to its presence the silence lost its tone of gloom, and a gleam of hope remained.

In the morning they continued their silent journey and split up when the snowy expanses ended at the side of Route 79. There they exchanged a few embarrassed jokes – jokes that were needed, because they had reached the end of their common journey and they felt a sense of respect and esteem for one another. It was a spirit of comradeship, something that had welded them together in the shack they had shared, and in the freezing days they had worked side by side. Now they all wanted to be off before a tear flowed down a cheek, or a voice trembled and failed. So they resorted to the method men have employed since the dawn of world history – humour.

Õunap suggested they could form a male strip-tease troupe, like the unemployed men in that movie. Goodluck Jeffersson thought that would be against his religion, and in any case Vatanescu's physique and Õunap's sense of rhythm militated against it.

Take care.

We'll meet again if we're meant to.

And so Goodluck Jeffersson took off in a westward direction, because there he thought he would find a skiing centre, a wife and a family, though his route might just as easily take him to Vittumainen Ghyll and Läähkimä Gorge. Urmas Õunap went to the east in order to implement his Plan B. His schooldays had left him only with bad memories and a knowledge of Russian he had never needed and had tried to forget. But up here in Lapland, Russian seemed to be a real advantage in the labour market, especially if you were looking for a job as a trail guide or second-home estate agent. From over the border flowed an endless stream of Russia's ever-growing middle class, with an equally growing urge to spend its money.

Where shall I go?

Guided by instinct, Vatanescu set off on foot south-ward, to Kolari. He reckoned that Lapland had nothing more to offer him, not even football boots. The berry-picking season was still six months away, and the reinvigoration of the reindeer business would take a generation or two.

Vatanescu walked up hill and down dale, he waded along motor sledge tracks, avoided the hotels and restaurants of Äkäslompolo and gave a wide berth to the unfinished holiday villages where in back yards prefabricated concrete slabs, polystyrene panels and piles of crushed stone – currently covered in snow – awaited the spring.

Then he found himself directly in front of a car that he recognised: Thomas Weissbier's Volvo XC90, rusting in the same place he had left it. Its owner had preferred to claim on his insurance and had bought a shiny new one. Such is the way of the world: goods have a purchase value, a sales value, an insurance value, a resale value, a sentimental value, a theft value, a scrap value and an exchange value.

What do I have that anyone would pay money for?

What do I have to give in exchange?

What guarantee can I offer?

Am I worth anything?

Vatanescu heaved open the door on the driver's side and attempted to start the engine. Not a sound, only silence and the steam of his breath in front of his face.

The rabbit jumped up to the windscreen, and its tiny warmth gradually thawed the frozen glass. It looked out of the opening, and then Vatanescu leaned right up next to it, so close that they could feel each other's insignificant and unique breathing, and gradually the hole in the ice became large enough for them to see the whole of the snowy, moonlit world.

Yegor Kugar needed a computer and an Internet connection. He had no money and Naseem Hasapatilalati did not want to mess up their friendship with loan agreements. Yegor remembered that his former employees had searched for their own clients on the Web, and he dragged his arse off to Vaasankatu Street to ring the intercom. Or rather, he climbed the fire escape to the balcony and entered the apartment that way. The former employee's name was Natasha. She had a client in bed with her, and there was a Toshiba laptop on the bedside table. Yegor told her to maintain her posture and look of boredom, and the client his red face, astonishment and erection. He put the Toshiba under his arm and scuttled back down to the street like a rat.

'The slut shouted from the balcony that things would go badly for me. That everyone knew I had no power any more.'

Yegor was perfectly aware of his situation. He knew that right from the outset he had been a social outcast, but in a very privileged position compared to others like him. Now he was in free fall towards a safety net that had a hole in it, a hole that grew bigger by the day. Yegor Kugar's entire career had been built on inspiring fear that inspired respect. Yegor was the wolf, others were the lambs.

Such is the fate of the crook, from the first day to the last. Few people begin with a desire to be a crook while they are still in the maternity ward. That point is reached through a series of chance events, great or small. In the case of Yegor Kugar, history's conveyor belt had once made a sharp turn, transporting him from the shores of the Arctic Sea to Vaasankatu Street.

No one would become a crook if they could obtain the same standard of living and pension by legal means. And even if one day they had enough money to be able to retire, at what point in their life would they jump off the train of criminality? A train that hurtles along at full steam, charged with electricity, through tunnels and into a brick wall. A bullet train. In two weeks of work a crook makes as much as a drive-in waiter earns in three years. The crook doesn't need to cringe before the system, to fill in forms or beg for a mortgage. True, the crook's world also has its systems and hierarchy, but, in his initial enthusiasm, the crook who is new to the game doesn't see that immediately. The crook finds himself in a family of other crooks, the drugs never run out, the jobs remain interesting. You make your own laws; the women are there for the taking, and you take them.

'Danger is hot, and it attracts the ladies; it's no good trying to explain it or turn it into something else. I even managed to screw a lot of female post-grad research students because they thought my animal nature, my violence and unpredictability made good subjects for research. Just like my penis, which is a lot longer than average.'

But now the wolf had been stripped of his fangs and his virility, his bankroll taken away, and the lambs had become wolves. Yegor Kugar was familiar with the practice, but he had never thought he would end up as a lamb. However, those were the facts. If that was how it looked, that was how it was, as an elder statesman would have said – and Yegor knew it too.

'I was going to end up as two lines in the local newspaper's crime bulletin: "*Russian killed in pedestrian underpass. Missed by creditors, and Natasha wants her laptop back.*"'

His forebodings were confirmed on the stairs outside his apartment. There Yegor Kugar saw three large leather-jacketed men. One of them bore an angle grinder and the other two had sledgehammers. They must have been there to retrieve Natasha's laptop, and that meant he had to beat a hasty retreat to the storeroom of Naseem Hasapatilalati's premises. Naseem said he was certainly willing to protect his only friend, but not at the risk of his own life. Yegor Kugar accepted the conditions.

Naseem Hasapatilalati brought Yegor Kugar meals and newspapers in his hiding place with a special coded knock. Otherwise the storeroom remained locked, and Yegor put shelves against the door. He knew what the Organisation's contract said; he had signed it in his own blood. You never left the Organisation on good terms, and even on bad terms there were only two options. Really bad or fucking bad. The first option meant surrendering all your worldly goods, and your little finger or your arm to the Organisation. The second option meant surrendering your life, and all that was needed for that to happen was for the Room Upstairs to find you dispensable. When the Organisation no longer had any use for a man like Yegor, a man like Yegor became a threat to it. He knew too much; he would start singing. The Organisation preferred to put an end to the singer's career before it even got started.

So Yegor Kugar's days were spent on his mattress in front of the open laptop. He did not search for porn or the ice hockey scores. Instead he searched for his erstwhile employee, his present arch-enemy, the Romanian beggar. And indeed he found him, in moving pictures, in material both free and paid for. The evening paper's placard had been only the start, for the search engine revealed the scale of the situation, producing more than a hundred thousand hits for the name 'Vatanescu'.

'With the help of Google Translate I managed to read the captions, though the photos themselves said enough. The guy kept popping up here and there with a face like a bag of spanners, but people were crazy about him. I really couldn't stomach the definitions of "Vatanescu" that were being thrown about:

'A symbol of downshifting.

'The saviour of a national treasure.

'Whaaaat?'

When Yegor Kugar noticed that Vatanascu had a lot of followers in social media, he joined Facebook himself. He wanted to test his own market value.

'I made one friend. Mama. She asked when I was coming home, because she'd run out of vodka. I clicked on LIKE. Then I replied, all right, Mamochka, I'll come, I'll come, just as soon as you reimburse me for a few things you forgot to give me in my childhood: love, security, warmth and food.'

After this experience Yegor Kugar found it hard to stomach the sight of Vatanescu's face when it appeared on YouTube, in the light topics at the end of the MTV3 news or on talk shows.

'Why did none of the news items ever call things by their name? He was a thief and a contract breaker. A Romanian swindler.

'And he was still carrying that fucking rat around with him, but it made them even crazier about him. He used it as a tearjerker, that thing. Plain über-dirty calculation. In the chat forums they thought he was something an advertising agency had come

141

up with, the guy who always happened to be in the right place. For the tree-huggers Vatanescu was a living statement of what a homeless vagabond ought to be."

But from Yegor's point of view the worst was still to come. He found it in the Russian newspaper where he checked the scores of his favourite ice hockey team.

Sanna Pommakka did not want to look after horses or be a nurse like the other girls in the first year at Puistola junior comprehensive. She wanted to deceive people, to take them in. She wanted to perform magic tricks. Sanna Pommakka wanted to make audiences rub their eyes and wonder how she did them, those tricks. That one? And especially that one?

In her local public library, in 1981, at the age of seven, Sanna Pommakka found a copy of *The Big Book of Magic* by Finland's best-known magician, Solmu Mäkelä, and at that moment she was certain that her future lay in the field of conjuring.

Sanna closed her fist on a handkerchief and when she opened it there were eight handkerchiefs there. She made coins disappear. She knew the number and suit of the cards her father thought of. She received the applause, the surprise and the wonderment for which she hoped. When on top of this Santa Claus brought her a Junior Magic Set, her happiness was almost complete.

But the approval and praise a child receives at home are deceptions, especially when compared with what takes place among their peers. Parents want their child to be happy, but by wanting it so much they make them unhappy later on. When Sanna showed off her talent at school, none of the other members of the class had any doubt about how the tricks were done. When the hidden coins fell out of Sanna's sleeve, Pertti in the back row burst into gleeful laughter. Pertti was given detention, but what was that compared to Sanna's sense of humiliation? The mere buzz of a fly in his ear.

Such is childhood: one wrong word, someone's laughter, one teacher's bad morning and the cruel assessment that follows, not even deliberate, but able to change the whole direction of a small person's life, removing hope and replacing it with despair.

Sanna Pommakka had been raised to have grand ideas about herself, but now she chose a path that was more assured. She had no ideas about herself at all. She would have no aspirations; she was going to stay a small, quiet person in the middle row, from the age of seven until she died.

Instead of magic tricks, Sanna Pommakka made ordinary existence, or rather survival, the focus of her life. She lost her virginity to Pertti in the back row, neither too early nor too late. Pertti was still laughing, not because he was cruel but because he was a sincerely stupid sixteen-year-old who had only three tools in his emotional toolkit: laughter, sarcasm and his fists. No magic at all in their shared moment.

Sanna's study supervisor thought her dream of college was unrealistic, so she went straight from junior comprehensive to work in a furniture store.

A year passed.

A fourth year passed.

The other employees continued their lives in further education or training, but Sanna remained where she was, and her fortnightly pay was enough for her to live on. She occasionally went out with Pertti from the back row, because he was always available and had a car with lowering springs. Though she didn't know what those were, they meant so much to Pertti that she respected them too.

When Pertti cheated on Sanna, Sanna thought it was her own fault. She wasn't good enough. Her looks, intelligence and character weren't good enough. She kept quiet about her own hopes and dreams because she was afraid that people would laugh at them, and as a result she would be rejected. So gradually her hopes and dreams died. Now her relationship with Pertti was over, and she had not seen him for three years.

Sanna Pommakka still delivered sofas and coffee tables and bunk beds to customers. The bigger the sofa, the more life there was in the house. Cots for infants, desks for schoolchildren, on rare occasions a rocking chair for an older person whose walls were decorated with photos of children, grandchildren and great-grandchildren.

One day Sanna Pommakka and her workmate delivered a corner sofa to a house in a residential area. The little boy who opened the door looked just like Pertti and laughed like Pertti – because he was Pertti's son. Pertti wasn't laughing any more, because he had a child in one arm and a wife in the other, and was now a good husband. Sanna Pommakka presented the delivery form, looked him in the eye and froze. The worst thing was that Pertti had obviously failed to recognise her, she reflected as she took his signature and returned to the furniture delivery van without a word.

It took six hours for the tears to come, and Sanna Pommakka herself didn't know why she was crying, alone on her own sofa, as a red-haired talk-show host made his live audience laugh with his introductory monologue.

The sofa store went bust. Because Sanna Pommakka had consistently put off joining the union, she was entitled only to the basic unemployment allowance. As severance pay she had received a sectional sofa that was far too big for her small apartment. She split it in two and gave half to her neighbours. Soon she had to split the remaining half, too, as her unemployment money was not enough to pay the rent, and she had to look for a place that was smaller and less expensive.

Sanna Pommakka's social exclusion did not happen suddenly or instantly; it was a gradual process that spread over time. In fact, it took place while she was asleep, because life was easier in dreams. There things happened, unlike in her waking life. Sanna had dreams of children jumping on their parents' double bed on a Sunday morning; she saw them in a large living room with a pine floor and wall-mounted bookshelves and toys on the floor, and in the corner a large TV set, and on the sofa a man whom she could love and who returned her love.

Sanna slept. When she woke she went out and bought frankfurters and fries at a 24-hour service station and ate dinner at three in the morning. Then she slept some more. When she finally woke up the day was far advanced. She watched soaps, dream garden shows, summer home property shows and drama series, and saw the full lives other people led. She also saw them on the news – in the kind of news where a woman had killed her husband, for the woman had a husband and they had children who would now have to be looked after. All these people's problems were connected with relationships. They had relationships in all directions, the world pulled them and pushed them and moved them about. Sanna's problems were exclusively her own. Chief among them was loneliness. Everything else flowed from that. Sanna Pommakka felt that she had been born into the world alone; alone she lived in it and alone she would leave it. And so what did anything matter?

Sanna lay on her one-third of a sofa and watched the renovation of the Nielikäinen family's three-room apartment. The children's bedroom was being given more space and painted white and the wardrobe cleverly expanded; the kitchen was being redesigned with the harmony of stainless steel and imitation marble tiles.

Sanna Pommakka ate cold sausage, and pined. Pining was wanting to be where one belonged without necessarily knowing where that was. It was where other people were. Where another person was, but how could she conjure that person up?

Only food made her feel better. The food had once been alive and it went inside her. In the course of a night Sanna could easily get through a kilo of fries and a couple of packs of frankfurters. The shelves of a German discount grocery store were her friends, her security, her source of surprise and understanding. For twenty euros she could fill a shopping bag with a wonderfully nurturing assortment of carbohydrates, proteins, sodium glutamate, sugar and salt. Sixty cents, it said on the red label of the pack of frankfurters that had passed their sell-by date.

Sanna changed the channel.

On the TV channel designed for men, a performing magician was being dropped into a deep, icy lake, bound with chains, locked in a box. Sanna picked up a fry. Sanna looked at the magician.

He believed in himself. He knew what he was doing, but no one else knew how he did it. He made people believe in him. His trickery worked.

Sanna Pommakka googled the man and checked up on his life. Wife a top model, two children, Mandus and Skylah. Sanna Pommakka suddenly had an awakening. Unlikely as it might seem, her energy had been returned to her by an illusionist named Germano Bully.

Sanna Pommakka travelled from the edge of town by metro, bus and train to the central library. In the library's entrance hall a miracle, a divine dispensation, a cinematic twist took place. Sanna Pommakka's eyes fell on a row of books that were being sold off cheaply, and the fourth one from the right was Solmu Mäkelä's *The Big Book of Magic*, one euro.

Such can be the price of one's future.

Sanna practised at home until she could do Solmu's tricks with her eyes shut, in the dark, suffering from serious sleep deprivation. At night school she enrolled in a magic class and also learned to take criticism as something that was aimed at her conjuring tricks rather than at her personally. In the follow-up class she received lessons in illusionism of a more sophisticated kind, as well as in how to manipulate one's audience.

The teacher claimed to have earned his own diploma in Las Vegas. He complimented Sanna on her swift hands and powers of concentration, but reproached her for her earnest expression, her over-sensitive peripheral circulation and her excessive weight. The magician was an entertainer, and for a woman that meant fake blonde hair and a wasp waist. She had to be at once practical and fuckable, the teacher explained.

Sanna Pommakka registered herself as a company and applied for a start-up grant. She made herself a website and applied for a pension. She got herself on the books of a small theatrical agency and accepted all the gigs she was offered, which at first only paid her expenses. She tested her tricks on her father and mother and asked them for once to be as honest as they could be with their only daughter.

'That one doesn't work,' said her father.

'Yes, it does,' said her mother.

'You're just saying that because you're my mum,' said Sanna.

'I saw the card up your sleeve,' said her father.

'You know, in the old days magicians used to lift rabbits out of hats,' said her mother.

In the People section of the weekend supplement of *Absolut Gazeta* there was an interview with a man named Harri Pykström. The photos had been taken from a helicopter, over the Lapland fells.

> 'A big fat Finnish ex-military type was explaining with a perfectly straight face what a great guy this Sicilian was, a real philanthropist. And at the side of the page it said that all Vatanescu wanted was football boots for his son.
>
> 'Bloody fucking hell! It's a lie! He wanted to destroy my life.'

So what did Yegor Kugar do about it? Did he lose his rag, did he drink a hundred cans of Sandels beer, did he start injecting drugs? Did he take a cab to Lapland to look for Vatanescu? Did he do what Yegor Kugar usually did in problem situations? Perceive the problem. Get rid of the problem. No, nothing like that. Yegor Kugar had lost his self-confidence. The neurotransmitters in his brain had gone on strike; he would have needed the help of a therapist, and third-generation antidepressants.

'I blame society and the system. It's too kind. It's too safe. This country is so safe that even a crook like the Yegor could afford to get depressed.'

Naseem Hasapatilalati suggested that Yegor should draw up a list of his problems, which would make them easier to deal with. Then perhaps he would be able to get rid of them, one at a time. Yegor picked up a sheet of graph paper and a pencil. Everything he wrote was about Vatanescu.

'As an employee he let me down. As a human being he let me down. He took the piss out of me. He let down the Organisation and I took the consequences. He pulled the rug from under my feet, and with it my future, my broads, my Beamer, my steaks, my friends and my mates. He took my life away. Thanks to him I became an outcast, an immigrant, a depressive without a future.'

The list only made it all worse. Vatanescu was penetrating ever more deeply into the convolutions of Yegor Kugar's brain, into his sweat glands and fear centre. In Vatanescu's case it was not a simple matter of a debt that had to be repaid or compensated with a little finger or a larger limb, or an apartment, a car or a wife if necessary. It was not just business, as 99.99 per cent of things in Yegor Kugar's life were.

Yegor Kugar understood his situation, and his problem concerning Vatanescu, when he saw a shaky video on the Web that had been taken with the camera of a mobile phone, showing the night emergency clinic at Maria Hospital. It zoomed in on Vatanescu and the rabbit that was sitting on his lap. The clip was hosted on an Israeli server.

'So that ugly mug was as famous as Jesus Christ, was he? What did that mean? It meant that this gutter's gift to the world had become what I was supposed to become.

'What was I supposed to become? A big shot. A star. A celebrity. An idol.'

Sanna Pommakka sat in the buffet car, crying. Or rather, her weeping could be compared to the thawing of someone frozen who had come in from outside. The ice turned to water, the water spilled over the table, someone spread a napkin on the pool of liquid. That someone was a dark-haired man wearing Repa-Rent overalls and a yellow cap, and he offered Sanna a napkin. Sanna accepted it. She looked the man in the eye.

I don't have a ticket.

They'll throw me off.

The place where I'm going is no more or less well known than any other in this country.

Sanna Pommakka glanced around her, sniffled and said something in the language of Finland. Vatanescu shook his head as a sign that he didn't understand.

'In deep shit,' Sanna said in English.

Me too.

'No money, no ticket.'

Tell me about it.

'I'm never going to get anywhere. Nothing ever works out for me.'

Vatanescu looked at her.

Lonely, fragile, human.

In the same train, human.

Vatanescu nodded to Sanna Pommakka like a psychotherapist, and in response Sanna whispered to him in a few short sentences how she came to be on this train. Two weeks ago she had received a brilliant job offer. A performer was needed for the opening of a new shopping mall. A woman. A blonde. Three thousand euros. It was such a lot of money that Sanna Pommakka had bought a pack of hair-dye with her Visa card and retrieved her exercycle from her parents' garage. With three thousand she could buy anything she wanted. An old car, good food, two months of safety. She could go on a trip somewhere. To Forssa, anyway.

Is Forssa in Italy?

It sounds like a beautiful place. A name full of power.

I'd like to go to Forssa some time. One day I will.

Sanna Pommakka gave a short laugh. An innocent man, perhaps even a good man. At any rate it was easy to sit opposite him. He didn't laugh at her, he didn't despise her and he didn't try to get into her pants.

Sanna Pommakka continued her story. She had flown in to Kittilä, where she was supposed to be picked up and driven to the shopping mall. But no one was there to meet her. She had called all the numbers that were written on the order sheet, but they were all unobtainable. She only had enough money for a taxi to the shopping mall construction site. When she got there she encountered workmen who had just been fired. The whole site had been closed down for eternity.

'I've been had,' said Sanna.

Vatanescu looked her in the eye. He put his hand on hers and lowered his gaze. The train was already in motion, and he put his yellow helmet on the table.

Sorry.

'It's not your fault. Whoever you are. Of course it's not. This is the way my life is, always has been, always will be; it's no good having any hopes because they always let me down.'

It is and it isn't.
My fault.

Sanna Pommakka sniffled and let Vatanescu hold her hand, even though he was foreign and came from warmer climes. His helmet trembled against the cutlery tray. On his overalls it said Repa-Rent, just like the world, everything for hire. Vatanescu noticed the metal-rimmed carrying case next to Sanna Pommakka.

Are you a musician?

'Magician.'

Of the meals that Naseem Hasapatilalati brought him Yegor ate only the rice, and growled. He neglected his personal hygiene, his hair and beard grew longer, and he no longer had the strength to crush all the silverfish that emerged from the drains. He, a man who had always gone forward, a man in whose view the analysis of the past was a task for wimps, no longer looked forward. Or back, or up or down. He looked inward; he was ready to live in his little closet until he wasted away. Perhaps that would indeed have happened if his rent agreement on the closet had not run out, but it did, and his living arrangements suddenly underwent a rapid – though not unexpected – change.

'I heard people rummaging in the closet next to mine and in the toilet. The rummagers were speaking my language, with the same accent: I'd performed enough of the same kind of evictions and door-to-door checks myself. At last they came to my store-room, but I had time to hide behind some banana crates.

'After closing-up time a sweating Naseem came to

explain that his cash till and display shelf of cigarettes had been cleaned out and that he'd been threatened with prolonged torture. He thought it was time
to say goodbye. Although he liked me, he liked his
life and limbs a fucking lot more. The Organisation
had given him twenty-four hours to denounce me. I
took my laptop under my arm and left the building.
It's not my way to beg for pity and mercy. Thank
you, I said to him, for the first time in my life.'

The Toshiba's battery still had two hours and fourteen
minutes of life left. Stopping in front of a café with large
windows, Yegor looked for a spot where he could get a
wireless Internet connection. He brought up the page
at vatanescu.com, where the photo at the top had once
again changed. Pykström and Vatanescu side by side,
with broad smiles on their faces, each with a bottle of
vodka under their arm, the rabbit bouncing about at
their feet.

'I became just Yegor the homeless guy, whom the
female down-and-outs pushed around while others
tried to steal the rags off his back. I took the last
tram at night or the first one in the morning to get
some peace. I could only ever get a patchy Internet
connection and the translation programme kept
hanging. Somewhere near Stockmann's department
store an item popped up which said that Finland's
most popular figure had acquired the dimensions
of a legend...

'That really got to me. A legend? Hello?

'Vladislav Tretyak is a legend and John Rambo
is a legend and Stalin and Vince Neil are almost
legends, but Vatanescu is about as much of a legend
as Co-op soap.

153

'I clawed at the tram seat. I'm ashamed to admit it, but I cried like an old woman. Then I asked myself a few questions. The answers had to be totally honest, for if I lied, I'd beat the crap out of myself.

'I'm a fair-minded guy, right?

'I want to be fair to people, right?

'Do I want to be a goddamn wanker?

'Don't I have the right to take the law into my own hands?

'Do I want respect?

'Do I have the means to take the law into my own hands? The strength? The will?

'Do I want broads?

'Do I have the courage to take what belongs to me? Or do I, Yegor Kugar, prefer to be a victim?

'Am I a victim?'

The ticket collector had plenty of genial chat for the passengers, and offers of a more personal nature for the girl who was serving at the buffet counter. They shared the same sense of humour, the same employer and possibly the same hated bosses. The girl poured the ticket collector a cup of coffee, and for another moment or two Vatanescu and Sanna Pommakka were able to travel in peace. The train was rattling through forests of dwarf trees, the electric cables hung low, and the trees bent humbly under their load of snow. On a motor sledge track the last group of tourists of the season, Dutch ones, were rolling along.

Let's go into hiding, Pommakka.

'Let's tell the truth.'

About what?

To whom?

Does the truth exist?

'In the first place, we have no money and no tickets.'

Maybe we can travel on credit. We'll do dishwashing. We'll massage people's shoulders. We'll perform somersaults. We'll melt the frost from the tracks.

Now it was Sanna Pommakka's turn to put her hand on Vatanescu's, without knowing why. Even though I do know, being the omniscient narrator who can get under the skin of his characters and rise up and observe them from the clouds if necessary. Sanna Pommakka took the initiative because Vatanescu posed no threat to her. He made no demands on her, did not want anything from her, she saw that right away. It might be a lack of ambition or willpower, but it could also be the sign of a purity and sincerity that were quite out of the ordinary.

'Secondly. Tell me who you are,' Sanna Pommakka said. 'Tell me the truth about yourself.'

If I knew it I would.

The ticket collector scraped the remains of the sugar from the bottom of his cardboard coffee cup with his spoon, and then crushed the cup and dropped it in the rubbish bin. With his reading device he inspected the tickets of two trade union officials who were on their way to Helsinki and, raising his cap slightly, wished them a pleasant journey. The men were red-cheeked; before each was a bottle of dark beer and a shot of schnapps. Their lives had a direction because the train had one. Straight on, and change at Riihimäki.

There were still several passengers between the ticket collector and Vatanescu and Sanna Pommakka. Sanna pressed Vatanescu's hand. He was showing signs of being about to flee.

'Don't leave me,' Sanna said.

Leave you? What? Who?

At that moment the rabbit stirred in Vatanescu's armpit.

Stay hidden.

Don't struggle.

Vatanescu stopped the rabbit's attempt to escape through his collar. Vatanescu stopped the rabbit's efforts to slip out of his sleeve onto the table. Sanna pressed the back of Vatanescu's hand so hard that it hurt. The rabbit navigated the obstacle and went down into the legs of his trousers, then along the edge of his safety boot and out.

The rabbit jumped into Sanna Pommakka's magician's top hat.

It jumped out of the hat.

It jumped into the hat.

The cardboard coffee cup rapidly filled with coins. Vatanescu handed the cup to the ticket collector and went to get another from the buffet counter. In between stations, Sanna Pommakka and the rabbit performed magic tricks, easily collecting the price of the next part of the way.

'Animals are not allowed in the buffet car,' said the ticket collector. 'But that one's something you need in order to do your job. It's not doing any harm.'

The tipsy passengers made generous donations, and soon five-euro notes were being thrust into Vatanescu's cup. Then a ten-euro note, followed by several more. There were even twenty-euro notes. Someone brought a pack of cigarettes, someone else a bar of chocolate, a third put down some luncheon vouchers, and one passenger parted with a paperback copy of a novel by Marko Tapio.

'Let's take a break,' said Sanna. 'My hands are numb.'

Vatanescu ordered chilli con carne for Sanna and himself, and milk and rye bread for the rabbit. Sanna was physically exhausted, while he was primarily astonished at his new role as impresario and magician's assistant.

'We make a good couple,' said Sanna Pommakka.

I had a wife once.

We thought we made a good couple. At least, I did. She wanted different things than I did, but she never told me what they were. I would have had to sense it.

I want football boots for my son.

'You respect me,' Sanna said.

You're a good magician and you get paid for your work.

You and the rabbit, you make a good couple.

Vatanescu put the coins into cups. There were now ten full cups, and two full of notes.

Over three hundred.

I can get football boots for my son.

Vatanescu and Sanna Pommakka left the buffet car and moved to the children's play area, where the little people were whizzing down a slide, making Lego, colouring pictures, scribbling, and hugging one another. And once again, as she did when delivering sofas to families with children, Sanna Pommakka felt at once moved and irritated. Not by the children, but by their parents. All kinds of emotionally crippled amateurs had spouses, former or present, and the sperm had fertilised the ovum without anyone asking questions. These people didn't know how to appreciate what they had, and instead of looking at their children they flicked through women's magazines with bored expressions, snapped at their spouses, stared out of the train window and thought about the life they should have chosen in place of their present one. Sanna Pommakka wondered the same thing as she was pulling the rabbit out of her top hat.

When the children noticed the magician, the yellow Repa-Rent helmet and the rabbit jumping out of the hat, popularity was assured. It was limitless. The show was a sell-out.

'You're good with children,' Sanna said to Vatanescu.

Yes. Why wouldn't I be? It's easy.

The children gathered at the feet of the trio. This meant that their parents' wallets and purses were open; all one had to do was help oneself. The children climbed onto Vatanescu's lap; they wanted to try his helmet on and play with the tools that still hung from the belt round his waist.

Keep them.

You have more use for them.

The children asked if Vatanescu had met Tractor Tom, and asked what kind of houses he built and if he was able to mend the plumbing without swearing. Because their dads weren't. Vatanescu didn't understand what the children were saying, but he got the meaning and the tone all the same. He sang them a song he had learned from his grandma Klara and the children put their own words to it. Sanna joined in too.

In the course of the evening Vatanescu noticed that the children's parents took just as many photographs with their mobile phones of him as they did of the rabbit. One or two passengers came to ask him for his autograph.

'It's really you,' they said.

Who or what do you think I am? Who do they think I am?

'I don't know,' Sanna said, and indeed she didn't. During all the time that Vatanescu had been growing into a media personality, Sanna had done nothing but practise her magic.

You think I'm someone else.

Someone important.

I'm not.

I'm Vatanescu, from Romania.

At midnight the working day was over and the passengers immersed themselves in sleep, their books or the music and movies on their laptops. Vatanescu and Sanna Pommakka divided the money and Vatanescu went off to ask the ticket collector for two sleeping compartments. After checking the reservations on his reading device, the ticket collector said there was only one sleeping compartment left.

'But it has three berths.'

I'm used to roughing it. I can sleep anywhere, as long as it's safe.

The rabbit and I will just sit up in an ordinary seat.

Sanna Pommakka told him not to indulge in self-pity or play the martyr. She was in the process of eliminating that sort of behaviour from her own life and from the layers of her mind, and she would do the same for the man from Repa-Rent. She ordered him into the compartment. Then she used the magic money to pay for tickets and sleeping berths all the way to the terminus. They still had eight hours to sleep before they reached Helsinki.

'We're partners.'

Partners?

'Business partners.'

Well, if you say so, then at least…

You take the lower berth.

As soon as the pair had gone into the sleeping compartment, the ticket collector gave the insatiable private and public media an update on their destination.

Vatanescu kicked off his overalls and hoped that the smell of his sweaty feet wouldn't carry excessively to Sanna Pommakka's nostrils. The rabbit wrinkled its nose and curled up on Vatanescu's pillow, under the night-light.

How long is it since I slept with a woman?

In the same room?

Sanna Pommakka removed her tailcoat, her bow tie and all her magician's accoutrements, and hoped that the odour of her underarm sweat would not carry excessively to Vatanescu's nostrils. She reckoned that she had earned almost the same amount as she had been promised for the opening show at the mall, a fat wad of banknotes of various colours. She would be able to pay the next month's rent and also the arrears. She was an artiste who had done her work and was sharing her sleeping compartment with a good man. The first man in her life with whom she felt at ease. With whom she didn't have to pretend, didn't have to make herself more or less than what she was. What was more, from a professional point of view the Rabbit-Vatanescu-Pommakka trio worked brilliantly, and one way or the other they would have to make it permanent.

'Perhaps we ought to perform in the street,' she said. 'Or on the trams, maybe. Gradually make a name for ourselves, like Birds of Lapinlahti?'

Birds of Lapinlahti?

'An intelligent rabbit, an intelligent woman and an assistant dressed like a building worker. A suitably strange combination.'

Do you have any children, Sanna Pommakka?

'No.'

I have a son, Miklos.

'It would be nice to meet him,' Sanna let out.

I'd like to meet him, too.

I don't know when that will be possible. I don't know anything about tomorrow.

Miklos has no reason to thank me for bringing him into the world if I'm not capable of giving him something.

An education. A future. Football boots.

'I wish there was someone I could have those sorts of thoughts about,' Sanna said in her own language, so that Vatanescu didn't hear it or understand it.

Are you asleep already?

Magician.

Her pyjamas in her arms, Sanna Pommakka looked at her reflection in the glass. This body, her private property, was no good; it excited no desire. Her breasts really didn't defy the force of gravity or form the kind of regular half-moons that would make a teenage lad lock himself in the train toilet in order to keep his hopes up on a paper towel. An appendix scar on her stomach, solid thighs that enabled the rest of her to stay upright. Her mind was more tricky: if it faltered, one day it would break. Into it came tomorrow, Helsinki's icy railway station, an unknown future, an east wind. Again to try alone, to foist herself on the magic market, to test her value. Trying to cope was all this life was about. The visit to the employment agency, the filling-in of the start-up application. The VAT accounts.

'I never want to spend another day alone.'

The ticket inspectors ordered the ticketless people smuggler off the train at Kisahalli, the Olympic

Sports Stadium. Yegor walked under Paavo Nurmi's statue, looked at the stadium tower and the people passing by and the morning drunks staggering out of the local cells. The laptop's screen showed a map of Finland and a blinking red dot that indicated Vatanescu's movements. At present the dot was somewhere on the outskirts of Hämeenlinna. In the latest pictures that had been added to the Web page, a woman named Sanna Pommakka was pulling a rabbit out of a hat held by Vatanescu.

'How is that any different from all the bunnies I've sold successfully around Europe? Someone ought to work out how many men a little Hungarian bunny cheers up during her twelve-hour working day. How her earnings compare to living at home in a slum with her parents on social security. Which doesn't exist anyway. Not to mention the effect of prostitution on the employment situation and the soft values it spreads. Getting your rocks off means less violence. There's no use denying it; it's been proved.

'The tastiest morsels are from Hungary. Their language is related to Finnish, but they come from a different gene bank from those Finnish cows with their legs like posts and their sagging breasts. The Hungarian whores have long legs, small but round buttocks – and the same goes for their tits. Sizzling hot and they know how to twitch their asses at the right time. And when they give blowjobs they don't mess about with condoms – that's quite a selling point in a country where people don't even dare to shake hands because one person caught bird flu. In Switzerland. Eighteen months ago. Coughs and sneezes spread diseases, did you wash them?

'And when I thought about all that I felt the old me coming back. Started getting it up again. Felt like screwing again. Began wanting things. Money and women and respect. They'd all been taken from me.

'I'm no victim.

'I make victims.

'I'm going to be a legend!'

Vatanescu's red dot was blinking somewhere around Kerava when Yegor's laptop battery ran out. He gave the laptop to a gentleman who had just been let out of the cells in a genial mood on account of his still being plastered. Then he tossed a coin to determine whether the beggar's journey had ended at Pasila or at Helsinki Central Station.

What are you doing?
Sanna.
Are you going to lie under the same blanket with me?
Pommakka.
We can't.
Yet you are.
Why shouldn't we? What am I pretending to be? I'm not a saint; I'm a human being.
I'm Vatanescu.
Yes, I'm lonely too.
Of course we can.
Come on.
You're…
…very…
…warm.

The rabbit hopped out from under the blanket of the lower berth onto Vatanescu's chest to be stroked. Sanna Pommakka snored beside him, and our hero was not embarrassed or ashamed in the slightest. Better to be two than on one's own. And three were even better. There weren't many Romanian beggars who had done it with a magician on a Finnish night train.

From the corridor there were footsteps and announcements. The stop at Tampere lasted a long time. Cars were being unloaded, tired-looking people walked in the lighted railway yard, torn from their sleep to begin their work, and a little boy ran about in such a lively way that he seemed not to know or care what time it was. Now was always a good time to be skipping around, and it was never too late to laugh or cry.

An empty mind.

A clear mind.

I know what I'm going to do.

What the task is.

Get shaved, put on my overalls and go to a sports shop like any other man.

Choose the football boots.

Pay for the football boots with the money the rabbit got for me by magic.

Pack up the football boots.

Post the football boots.

Buy a phone.

Call home.

Life is an opportunity.

I feel that now.

I'm going to manage.

I'm going to buy an apartment, rent an apartment, two rooms, tiling, constant hot water, bright lighting.

I'm going to buy a car, an old banger that costs a thousand euros, which I will drive wherever I choose. I will phone this woman who's sleeping beside me, and I'll invite her to the cinema. I will tell her about me, and she will tell me about her. We'll get to know each other and eventually I'll introduce her to Miklos, and even to my family.

Could that be possible?

Vatanescu searched in his overalls and found what he was looking for: a piece of chocolate wrapped in foil. He was in the process of unwrapping it when Sanna Pommakka woke up. She looked at Vatanescu tenderly, without anxiety or forlornness, or the sense of emptiness she usually felt in the mornings.

'Good morning.'

Would you like some chocolate?

'Mmm... where are we? Shall we go and eat somewhere when we get to Helsinki? We still have money.'

Almost there.

'Are we going to stay... I mean, are we going to travel together?'

Where?

'Somewhere. Where are you going?'

To a sports shop.

'I'll come with you... Vata. I'll come to the sports shop with you.'

Vatanescu sucked his chocolate, for if it got into the hole in his right molar, the pain would only go away if he took a handful of painkillers.

Sanna Pommakka drew Vatanescu towards her and put her head on his chest.

It would be even better if there were someone who would buy the football boots for me.

Someone with a loyalty card. Do you have a loyalty card?

'Yes.'

With points on it?

'Yes, I do.'

A social security ID, a phone number, a fixed address?

'Of course I do, dear sir.'

And then Vatanescu and Sanna Pommakka packed up their things, but drew the curtains of the sleeping berth again for the journey between Järvenpää and Helsinki. If Vatanescu had a dominant feeling, it was one of languor. For Sanna Pommakka, it was self-confidence. Their paths had crossed when they were poor, unemployed and disrespected, but now they had a future ahead of them. The group would not be complete without the rabbit – and its dominant feeling was one of secret jealousy.

Vatanescu and Sanna Pommakka could now hold their heads up as they entered society – a part of it anyway, or at least its fringes. They joined the ranks of those whose lives were in order, who could pay their monthly debts, afford a new car every three years, afford to let their children go riding, play the drums or do messy finger-painting, and praise them again and again, even though a mess was really just a mess.

Sanna Pommakka wondered if she could enter that world with this man. Vatanescu's mind was mainly on the football boots, but he also enjoyed the scent of Sanna Pommakka's hair.

They stood by the door in single file, the train slowed down before it stopped, and even though they might never be a couple, they would always share the magic of the Kolari–Helsinki night train.

A film star's reception awaited Vatanescu. Cameras, mobile phones, autograph books, the media and production companies. One woman wanted his signature on her breasts, another on the side of her baby, a man on his 1 Percent waistcoat.

The crowd forced its way between Sanna Pommakka and Vatanescu. First they lost each other's hands, then they could no longer see each other. Sanna shouted her address, which Vatanescu failed to store in his memory.

We'll meet again if we're meant to.

'How do you feel now?' asked a sports correspondent.

Is this how they celebrate when a man meets a woman and gives up being alone in order to be together?

Are you all crazy?

Little girls plucked hairs from Vatanescu's head, little boys admired his workman's overalls. He saw T-shirts covered with pictures of himself and the rabbit. On the quayside there were hastily improvised stalls selling Vatanescu-themed spin-offs. There were people dressed as rabbits and people dressed as beggars.

Madness.

Step aside, please...

...would you let me through...

...I need to find a sports shop.

Then Vatanescu sensed a figure in the human ocean. He sensed it without seeing it yet, sensed it on his skin, like electricity. The figure was pushing its way determinedly through the mass of people; it was heading straight for him, like the blocks of ice careering down the River Kyrö in the spring.

I must
run
away.

I must
protect
the rabbit.

The event has been recorded by numerous witness statements and on lots of CCTV footage, but there was only one perpetrator and one victim.

'I pushed the crowd of people in front of me apart with two hands as if they were sliding doors. Layer by layer, eight inches at a time. They were all in a crazy state of mass hysteria, but my task was to restore order. I kept the blade behind my arm and knew that the surest way would be to make a quick stab to the throat the way it's done by the mujahedin, or whatever those skirt-wearing Jedi warriors are called. It was just a question of whether I could get close enough to Vatanescu to step behind him.

'I, Yegor Kugar, was back.

'I was on the warpath, I was going to become a legend.

'We'll see which one of us will be written about after this!'

Now I died.

Chapter Nine

*In which we make the acquaintance of Finland's prime
minister, and in which Vatanescu awakes from the dead*

Finland's prime minister Simo Pahvi sat in the café of
the Neste service station near Eläintarha Park with
his driver Esko Sirpale. They were waiting for a third
man.

'These chairs are no good,' Pahvi said. 'They're
designed for backsides. I have an arse.'

Today was the day that Simo Pahvi's party was to
define its future. Its values, strategies and direction.

It had all begun forty years earlier with the founding
of the Ordinary Smallholders' Party by Simo Pahvi's
predecessor and mentor, Heikki Hamutta. The party
had been his life's work. Depending on one's point
of view, and which political correspondent one read,
Hamutta had been either a dissident, an enemy of the
state, a troublemaker, a loudmouth or a saviour. In his
own opinion Heikki Hamutta knew the people, trusted
the people and wanted to help the people. He had grown
up among the people, was a product of the Karelia that
had been abandoned to the Russians. The door of the
lift to the upper echelons had been open, but Hamutta
preferred to go by the stairs and the gravel roads.

Heikki Hamutta had made it his mission in life to
fight for the big issues of the little man. In a big world he
took the little man's side against big enemies. Against
the bosses, the communists, big domestic capital, big
foreign capital; all the forces that tried from all directions

to encroach on the land of the rural smallholders and take away what little they had. The threats did not have to be real – it was enough that they appeared real in the smallholders' minds, and that they were updated at regular intervals. Heikki Hamutta wanted to breathe new life into a section of the population that had been thought to be either dead or asleep.

Little by little, he had turned the small party into a big one, and talk had become more important than deeds. Words. Figures of speech. A lively and ready wit. Clear-cut sentences, tinged with humour. There had to be bite, but no irony. No detours, no circumlocutions, nothing too off-topic or airy-fairy. Then the audience wanted to hear more.

'The man people want to hear gains a voice,' Hamutta had said. 'The man people want to hear gains a face. The man who acquires a face gains visibility. He's in demand in the newspapers, on radio and TV. He gains votes in their hundreds of thousands.'

Simo Pahvi had heard the voice of Heikki Hamutta in a shopping mall in a remote suburb of the capital during the years when brown and yellow were fashionable and colour TV was in its infancy. Pahvi sat on the saddle of his bicycle eating a vanilla Eskimo ice cream and thinking a boy's thoughts: the maximum speeds of cars and Superman's chances in a fight with Lex Luthor.

Then a portable amplifier crackled into life and the deep voice of the little man was heard. Heikki Hamutta was explaining what was wrong with the world and how to put it right.

Simo Pahvi had immediately joined the party and told his parents about his new plans for a future career. Gone were his dreams of being an engine driver or a fireman; he wanted to be a politician. A minister. Prime minister.

Pahvi was struck by Hamutta's power with words, his sense of rhythm, his timing, his ability to communicate with the public and instinctively grasp its mood. Hamutta's policies were a side issue – important, it was true, but if they had been presented to Pahvi in a different form, in stammering phrases or academic language, their effect would have been nil.

This was Simo Pahvi's first illumination.

He had found his path and his life's purpose at the age of nine. He had bought an ill-fitting suit at a cheap department store, and still did so – a new suit every ten years. He bought large non-prescription glasses and gave up playing football because he wanted to look more imposing. That meant a more generous waistline and a double chin, the kind one has to have if one intends to be a politician on radio and TV.

Simo Pahvi earned Hamutta's trust by arriving at meetings with telephone directories, which he sat on in order to make himself the same height as everyone else. He did the same on the speakers' platform, and got the most applause after Hamutta. Such strength of will in a boy not yet ten promised him a great future in the Ordinary Smallholders' Party. What was more, Heikki Hamutta recognised the need for a mascot: with the help of a small boy one could gain extra points for warmth and humanity.

Pahvi absorbed all the characteristics of his role model, both outer and inner – his skill as a public performer, his pithy rhetoric, his benevolence towards his own, his steadfastness in the face of opponents and injustices.

So it continued for twenty years. Pahvi gained a reputation among his peers and rose to be number two in the party organisation. That was all anyone knew about him. He stood for parliament, but did not get in. Not discouraged, he went on being Heikki Hamutta's trusted companion.

He toured the countryside with Hamutta, now on a tractor, now on a moped, sometimes on a bus invariably driven by another man who enjoyed Hamutta's confidence: his driver Esko Sirpale.

The party's supporters opened their homes for evening meetings, where the business of the Ordinary Smallholders' Party was discussed late into the night, with never an eye on the clock. Improvements were promised. Householders offered guests refreshments and a place to stay for the night. At the end of one such evening Simo Pahvi was preparing to bed down when the daughter of the house brought him something for his heartburn.

There she was. His wife and mother of his children. Simo Pahvi was a plain-talking man of conservative tastes, so he lost no time in proposing to Marjatta. In the morning he asked her father for permission to marry her, and a month later they were husband and wife. Two months later Marjatta was expecting their first child.

Just as a new life was growing inside Marjatta, Heikki Hamutta's life came to an end. Cancer of the prostate, old age, all the miles he had driven and walked and struggled finally claimed their own. For this, Pahvi had not been ready. No one is ever ready for such a thing – when the head of an establishment, an ice hockey team or a company grows too powerful. When such a leader passes away, all that remains of him are his boots, which don't fit any of his successors. They are not able to walk in them, those boots; they don't know where they let in or what to do about the leaky soles.

It was also around this time that the smallholdings and their owners finally disappeared from the land.

There was nobody left, and no causes to defend any more. Heikki Hamutta died. The party went bankrupt. Many thought its ideals had died, too.

At the age of thirty-three, Simo Pahvi realised that he was an unemployed political hopeful. He realised it as he was filling his car at the Weathervane service station in Häme. Without enough money to fill the tank, he didn't know what direction to take. He had forgotten where he had come from and had no idea where he was going, either in terms of his journey or of his life as a whole. Now that he was out of work, the glasses he had bought to give himself political credibility, the ill-fitting suit and the extra inches round his waist merely made him look like a drifter. He had put Heikki Hamutta's boots in a crate in the basement of his apartment building, but had not even dared to look at them.

Simo Pahvi wondered what his unborn child would think of a father who after doing the football pools fills out an unemployment benefit form. As he got back into his car after paying for his petrol he was close to a crippling dose of self-pity. But on the slip road into Route 4, Simo Pahvi had the second illumination of his life.

At the side of the road stood a hitchhiker. As a rule he did not give lifts to hitchhikers, but for once there was room in the car and he had the time to spare. He reached over and opened the door on the passenger side.

'Where are you going?' he asked.

'I might ask you the same question,' the man replied.

'Lahti.'

'You booked me,' the man said.

'Not to my knowledge...'

'I'm Jesus.'

'Jesus?'

'Jesus Mähönen, hi. Tell me now, what's up, friend?
Where is your road taking you?'

Pahvi put the car into first gear and accelerated.

'Nowhere in particular. I thought I'd take a drive
somewhere. Maybe to Mikkeli.'

'Wrong. You're going home, they need you there.'

Pahvi looked at the road ahead of him. He looked at
the crushed squirrels that lay at its edges, the carcases
of raccoon dogs, and a man who was pushing a bicycle,
its pannier full of empty bottles. He saw the radio masts
and ski-jumps of Lahti, and asked Jesus to repeat what
he had said.

'They need you at home.'

It was true, if he knew what home was. Home was
Marjatta and home was the party.

'You'll make a U-turn at the next intersection and
you'll head for home.'

And Simo made a U-turn and headed for home.

'In the next few days a child will be born to you,' said
Jesus Mähönen. 'Take care of it. And after it, everything
else. You will show people the way. You are life's traffic
cop. The traffic cop of domestic politics. You must know
whom to stop at the red light, whom to let through at
the green. Which route is clear, which route may have
delays. And which route has a wide transport truck that
can't be overtaken for twenty miles.'

Pahvi said that he often didn't understand his own
metaphors, and so Jesus must explain himself more
clearly.

'Have faith in your own abilities, Pahvi. Only then
will you become a figure in Finnish politics who is
greater and more legendary than Heikki Hamutta. Do
you understand?'

Simo Pahvi thought about it.

174

'Think, man. Think, but don't get hung up in your thoughts. Make a decision. Good or bad, a decision is always better than being in limbo. You can let me out here, at Keimolanportti.'

Pahvi left Jesus at the local service station, and although I am the omniscient narrator, I cannot say if this really was the Saviour, or simply Jesse Mähönen who had recently escaped from the mental hospital at Kellokoski. In any case it does not matter, as by their very definition questions of faith involve a consonance not with reality, but with faith.

On his way home Pahvi dropped in at the super-market. He served celebratory coffee, accompanied by a litre of vanilla ice cream with instant chocolate sauce. His wife asked him what they were celebrating, as only yesterday he had been in the depths of misery and despair.

'Procreation,' Pahvi replied, and in his voice for the first time there was that tone of vigour that would make him famous in times to come. 'A piece of me is growing inside you, Marjatta. Tomorrow I'm going to order five thousand cards for the party's members.'

'Which party?'

'My party. The Ordinary People's Party. Will you take cream?'

Support for the party began at zero. Now it had reached thirty-three per cent. Gradually, with the help of mannerisms he had learned from Hamutta, methods he himself had devised and the tips he received from Jesus, Simo Pahvi's laid-back assertiveness found its way into the consciousness of the entire nation. After Ozzy Osbourne, Simo Pahvi was the second person in the world to prove the truth of the maxim 'being your-self is enough'. Most of us have to make a real effort to be more than ourselves if we want to achieve more than making our morning porridge. To be oneself is often to be a repulsive pariah, an obnoxious chatterer, a complacent bastard, a sneering idiot, a bimbo, a cretin, an irresponsible Don Juan, a timorous creep, a sneaky abortion – at any rate something that elicits no answering echo anywhere.

Simo Pahvi's answering echo came from the markets, the farms, the pubs and the pedestrian underpasses. It came as a full-throated shout. Simo Pahvi's identity was that of Uncle Veijo. The man who says, enough of all this talk, let's get on with the job. Who dares to stand up and leave the table saying that if that guy utters another word of crap we'll all down tools. When Simo Pahvi took the lead you were ready to follow him, to go to the village dance, to work in Sweden, to brawl in bars, fight the Winter War, the Continuation War and the Civil War, and attend church at Christmas.

You had to be close to the voters. To touch them, get under their skin. Within reach of a stained cup of coffee or a can of beer brought back from Tallinn. In summer around the barbecue, passing the packet of sausages, in the thirty square feet of the garden of a rented urban terraced house. That was where Pahvi had come from, that was where he went, and that was where he derived the rationale for his policies and his life.

It was in being himself that he had suffered defeats and scored his victories. That he had worked the turf and got to know his voters. Although one didn't get to know people just by shaking their hand, Pahvi was able to draw conclusions and generalise, but in such a way that each person felt they were being individually addressed. The points that mattered were: what did someone lack? What could fill the gap? Should one promise what was really lacking, or something else? Put the blame on what was wrong or transfer it onto some quite different, externalised problem? Who was to be held responsible for the faults and omissions?

Simo Pahvi gave himself the image of someone who could diagnose the problem and would come back next summer to put it right. A broken gutter. Squeaky brakes. A firm's relocation abroad. Unemployment. Pensions that were too small. Immigrants.

In those who voted for him, the figure of Simo Pahvi kindled the hope of being like Simo Pahvi. The distance from Pahvi to the people was so short that the ballot box was only a step away, and the right number was invariably chosen on the ballot paper.

Pahvi added slight deviations to his ordinariness. He wore an ordinary quilted jacket that smelled of tobacco smoke, motor oil and kebab sauce, but also a green scarf that was quite out of the ordinary: Simo Pahvi was a supporter of the Swedish football team BembÖle FIS. His enthusiasm was genuine, dating from his honeymoon in Uppsala, but the scarf was a deliberate test of the flexibility of his political support. If people accepted his unusual choice of football team, then in difficult situations they might also accept any other unusual choices and directions he might take. He was careful not to define his political leanings too narrowly. If one kept a certain freedom of action, one could go on drawing support from new sections of the public. And, just as he had calculated, the scarf put the finishing touches to the caricature.

The other touchstone was Jesus Mähönen. In an interview for *Smile* magazine, Pahvi said that he knew Jesus personally and often consulted him when making decisions that affected his private and political life. This, too, the public and the media had accepted, because the statement was interpreted as metaphorical. When Pahvi was unable or unwilling to answer some question related to the budget, for example, he would say:

'I'll have to ask Jesus first.'

His supporters would burst into laughter. His political rivals were surprised at the way he always landed on his feet. If they said the same things, they would be viewed as symptoms of mental illness.

'Three words are enough to change the world. The thing is to know what those three words are.'

This precept of Heikki Hamutta's was one that Pahvi always remembered.

In the third round of the parliamentary elections the Ordinary People's Party had won a so-called 'tsunami' victory. In their use of this term, the political correspondents wanted to emphasise that the landslide had gone far into the depths of the country, overturning and upsetting everything, but would also come crashing back, returning some of the ordinary people who had risen to become members of parliament to their original status of sawyers, postmen, unemployed paper mill workers, students, border guards, policemen and checkout assistants.

The party was aware of the risk, and for the next election campaign a group led by Pike Salomaa, a world arm wrestling champion, even wanted the Ordinary People's Party to try an independent PR agency.

Simo Pahvi often said in public that he listened to and trusted all who were wiser than himself. But Pike Salomaa was not one of them. Even though he had brought in the votes of the women and arm wrestlers of south-west Finland. In reality Pahvi thought that no one was wiser than himself, and that only Jesus and his driver Esko Sirpale were on his level.

But he knew that no leader should ever become too powerful or irreplaceable. If you took all the power for yourself, you began to find enemies in your own kitchen.

The reason for Simo Pahvi's success was Simo Pahvi. The reason for Simo Pahvi's problems was Simo Pahvi.

Simo Pahvi went to the counter and got himself a refill of coffee.

Simo Pahvi took a bite of his doughnut, the fifth of the day, and slurped down some coffee after it. He told Esko Sirpale that he could see no one among the ranks of the Finnish people who would be capable of stepping up to stand before them as leader. He pulled a pack of cigarettes from his pocket. Esko Sirpale did the same. They threw the cigarettes into the rubbish bin and opened out the cardboard packs. A cigarette pack was Simo Pahvi's laptop and drawing board. This was how he had designed his summer cottage, his career, his wedding, his campaign budget and his EU policy. Everything was planned according to the same principles. Foundations that were damp-proof. A solid structure and a well-aired loft. Proper sheet iron on the roof, no aluminium foil.

'What are we designing?' Esko Sirpale asked.

'A strategy.'

'We're not going to use a PR agency?' Sirpale asked. 'We're going to do it ourselves?'

'It's not the work that hurts your back, but the bending.'

Then Pahvi stirred his cup of coffee with his spoon, not saying a word.

'Is there a problem?' Sirpale asked.

'A big one,' Simo Pahvi sighed. 'The problem is that I've got all I ever wanted.'

'Yes, you have. Thumbs up, and congratulations.'

'I've been made a minister,' Pahvi said. 'All my aims have been fulfilled.'

Simo Pahvi's gaze wandered along the enclosure of the Eläintarha sports stadium and past a woman in blue overalls who was filling a Ford Transit van.

'Exactly,' Esko Sirpale said. 'Bloody hell. Let's not mope about it.'

'I'm empty.'

It took Jesus Mähönen three minutes to cycle from his apartment to the service station. As he didn't drink coffee, he asked for a cup of hot water.

'Please speak,' Jesus asked.

'I'm an old-fashioned man. I don't do the vacuuming. I don't count the calories. I support responsibility, not liberties.'

Jesus and Esko Sirpale nodded and asked him to continue.

'I've lost faith. In the future.'

'Has something happened?'

'No. I'm going to win the presidential election.'

Jesus and Esko Sirpale nodded.

'But when I get to the president's office, someone will have to take orders. Who, damn it?'

They were silent. Behind them old Irma got three watermelons on the fruit machine and won a hundred euros.

'I'm the Ordinary People's Party.' Pahvi said. 'But this morning on the john I realised that an ordinary person can't lead the Ordinary People. I thought that he could, but he can't. An ordinary person wants power, not responsibility.'

'It's good that you've realised it,' Sirpale said. 'Like Hamutta.'

'That's what people are like,' said Pahvi. 'But if you give power to someone who covets it, you're going to end up a very long way from the original idea of the Ordinary People's Party. My successor must be the One, with a capital O.'

Simo Pahvi finished his coffee, and thought. He got another refill and drank that, too. He went on thinking, looked at his trusted men and listened to his innermost self.

'I've never had any doubts. Now I do. I don't want to lose my life's work.'

'But you want to be president?'

'If I don't run, I will always regret it. But the party needs a good man to lead it. Someone who won't let us down. Who won't fire guns when he's drunk. Who won't line his own pockets. Who won't come out with stupid statements on TV. Who won't say openly what he thinks about blacks, homosexuals and abortion. Who won't support the death penalty until the time is ripe. Who can talk about the bosses, the waste-water reform and the EU. He must be a new man, a man who is wise. Yet close to ordinary folk. Able to understand them. Aware of current trends. Not out for his own success.'

Simo Pahvi said nothing for a long time. Jesus Mähönen said nothing for a long time. Esko Sirpale whistled to himself and put his hands behind his head.

'You see,' Pahvi said. 'There isn't anyone like that.'

'Of course there is,' Sirpale said. 'If history has taught us anything, it's that no job remains vacant for long.'

Jesus Mähönen nodded in agreement.

'Show me the way,' Pahvi demanded. 'Tell me where I can find a man like that.'

And Jesus told him.

His perpetual motion stopped on the seventh floor of Meilahti Hospital, in an intensive care ward with special surveillance

I can feel the stitches in my side.

I'm full of holes.

So this is the end of a wonderful life, then?

I don't know if it's daytime or night-time, I'm being fed through a tube.

The policemen took three shifts in turn. There was always someone on guard.

To watch me?

To protect me?

From whom?

It was Yegor.

Did they arrest him?

The medication gives me strange dreams.

I dream about Harri Pykström picking mushrooms in the forest with Arto the writer.

They're waving to me from the other side of the river.

I go to join them. To a quad bike, a boat, a bottle, a sauna, to float logs, to build factories, hurl lightning, give the Son of Man a brotherly pat on the back. Men's work. Real jobs.

A man.

Am I a man?

Is that what I am?

What sort of man is it who can't get a pair of football boots for his son?

When Vatanescu was able to speak, he asked first about the rabbit. No one had any firm information, but the policeman said he was afraid it might have ended up as tiger food at Korkeasaari Zoo. He promised to investigate the matter.

If the rabbit dies, I will die.

'Now, don't let's exaggerate. Everything will be all right.'

If I die, the rabbit will die.

If I'm deported, they'll kill me.

The medication kept the pain at bay, but it also affected Vatanescu's mind, which swayed and undulated. He had lost all sense of time and place, and grey specks and graphic elements swam before his eyes. He asked if there was any news of Sanna Pommakka, but the name was not familiar to the hospital staff.

Did she never exist at all?

Do I?

Each day a doctor checked his condition to see if he could now be interrogated and the process of deportation begun.

At last the day came when Vatanescu was able to eat unaided. Raised up in his hospital bed, broth and sour milk.

'You're in trouble with the taxman. You had a wild animal with you, which you took into restaurants, an employment agency and a hospital. You performed magic tricks on a train without an entertainment licence. You took part in an unsanctioned demonstration...'

As a punishment Vatanescu received day-fines and was told he would be deported back to where he had come from. He could take with him only what he had arrived with.

Nothing.

I had nothing.

The football boots would have been enough.

'Perhaps there's an alternative.'

I haven't any money. I can't offer any bribes.

'Your crimes are worth peanuts. There's one thing that is important.'

The rabbit.

'Kugar. You're our only witness against him. What was your connection with him?'

If I tell them I may get off lightly.

If I tell them I may die.

'What do you mean, Vatanescu?'

Even if Yegor goes to prison, there are others like him who will continue his activities. His post won't stay vacant. It will be filled in the blink of an eye.

To that gang I will always be a stool pigeon.

'How long have you known Kugar, Vatanescu?'

A dead stool pigeon.

'He's a human trafficker, a drugs trafficker and an arms trafficker. You've no reason to protect a man like that.'

No, but I must protect myself.

And my child. And my mother.

'We know that... your sister...'

My sister?

'...is safe. In a refuge. A clandestine brothel was uncovered in Poland; all the girls are safe. But she left Romania in the same group as you, and her testimony will also be useful to us. We can guarantee to protect your family.'

You?

You personally?

A Finn? You can protect my family in Romania?

'Yes. Or here. As you wish.'

Yegor Kugar was driven to a cell at Pasila police station and from there to a maximum-security prison somewhere in the wilds of Finland. Captivity did not dismay Yegor Kugar; he was calm, had obtained his revenge, accomplished his mission. The handcuffs did not hurt him, the Finnish prison system had the softness of the womb. In Finland, prison was an easier and more decent option than freedom in most other countries. So every-thing had worked out fine for Yegor Kugar – or had it?

'Damn damn damn damn damn fucking damn! The beggar wasn't dead. Between yours truly and Vatanescu it was a question of market value, and I had tried a little takeover bid. Even that went tits up.'

In prison Yegor Kugar encountered a hierarchy where only a rabbit-killer occupied a lower status than that of the sex offenders. For like the rest of the country the prison population had followed the journey of Vatanescu and the rabbit, and it had brought solace to their lives. From Vatanescu's free roaming as a vaga-bond they derived hope. In him they saw what might be possible. A man who had broken away from society and even then had become successful, gained the undivided attention and respect of his contemporaries.

At his very first meal, Yegor Kugar had to defend himself with a tray and a cup of hot coffee. Screwdrivers came at him from two directions, and only the swift intervention of the guards saved him.

Yegor Kugar wanted to be put in isolation, and put in isolation he was. The man who could not sleep alone now preferred to be as alone as it was possible to be in this world.

'I saw it as a chance for spiritual growth. So that when I eventually got out I'd be both softer and harder in the right proportion. I didn't stick porn pictures on my walls like the wankers in the neigh-bouring cells. I wanted the real thing, or nothing at all. And I wasn't taking the train to brown town either. It's a matter of smells, curves, softness and contrasts. Chasing some George in the next cell who was just the same cold-balled shit as I was, no thanks. I need to get the skin, the smell, the frizzy hair, the titties, the original heat of rutting sex, I need to tickle the nipples till they're upright and then go to the limit, nearly to the point where I come. And stay like that for half an hour or so. And only then let the sauce fly.

'But anyway, why do I write stuff like this? I'm getting a hard-on. And I don't know why anyone would want to publish it.

'My screwing was over and gone.

'And my time had not yet been done.'

Thus did Yegor Kugar moulder and meditate in his solitary cell, coming out to stretch his legs for half an hour once a day, gazing at the walls and the sky. Yegor Kugar had no aims in life. Just one wish.

'The worst thing would have been for me to be sent back into the arms of my motherland where they would dig up all kinds of things – in addition to my knifing the beggar. I definitely wanted to remain a client of the Finnish prison system.

'I tried to find Jesus. I stuck an icon on the wall, but I couldn't see anything in it. I got a telly; I could see a lot more on that, but of course there were those goddamn daily reports on Vatanescu's health. They remembered to show my name and my mug and to say that the stabbing had become a serious diplomatic incident.

'On the news there was never anything about my background, I hadn't told anyone anything, and I'd been wiped from the files of the security police, that's for sure.

'During my questioning I played the role of a real idiot, saying, I dunno, and what's that, and eh, how should I know.'

In his solitude Yegor Kugar began to write his memoirs. At first in secret on graph paper, because he imagined it was forbidden. When a friendly warden from Askola saw what was keeping Kugar busy, he got him a typewriter and paper.

'I want to tell this story of mine for one simple reason: so that no one will ever go down the road that I did... My ass. I'm doing it for the money. I could get a book deal. Or *Bild* might want to publish an exclusive interview with me. It wouldn't be bad if a 7 Series BMW was waiting outside the prison for Yegor Kugar, as it ought to be. I think the Finns ought to be giddy with anticipation for *Memoirs of a People Smuggler*, seeing how they lap up all those ramblings by old homos, lesbians and heteros about their cultural struggles. I dare to believe that the true struggles of a true Russky would find a place in the Christmas book market.'

As Yegor Kugar wrote, his case went forward. The trial was held in an air raid shelter, far away from anywhere, as it was suspected that international crime stood behind Yegor Kugar, and there were fears that too public an occasion might bring the noiseless helicopters and noisy SWAT teams of certain countries to land on the premises of the court.

'I got the best lawyer there was, a guy named Limpola. He said he was sorry he hadn't been alive when the Nuremberg trials were on, as he would have loved to defend Nazis. Out of pure provocation. And almost in the same breath he told me he was one-quarter Roma. Out of pure provocation. I couldn't have cared less, as long as the guy got me a lighter sentence, i.e. a better deal. After all, that was business, too, to let them know what sort of agreement, based on the prevailing conditions, we could accept.'

But even the best lawyer was to no avail, because one night the hour of Yegor Kugar's departure arrived. The diplomatic negotiations had reached their conclusion, and it was time to fetch the boy home. Were the men from the security police or were they from the Organisation? Probably both, wearing two hats. A black hood was placed on Yegor Kugar's head, and the warden from Askola could only stand by and watch.

'Someone had grassed me up good and proper. Vatanescu had told them what I'd been doing. I was whisked off home before I could appeal to international justice. Hopefully I will at least get my name in large letters. In the tabloids. On the Web. On my gravestone.'

When Vatanescu's wounds had healed up, he was moved from intensive care to a normal ward. A plain-clothes policeman remained in the corridor to guard or protect him, depending on whether he tried to leave the ward or someone else tried to get in. The days were long, the future uncertain, but fortunately there was a television set where he could watch endless amounts of news and decent football.

To Vatanescu's bedside came a man and a woman – a CID detective and a mediator from the immigration office. They held out a document which said that Vatanescu was to be deported to his homeland.

You promised... That man. The one who interrogated Kugar.

'I don't know about any promises others may have made.'

He promised my sister.

My mother.

My rabbit.

The man told Vatanescu that he ought to be glad he had got off so lightly. There were quite a number of charges against him.

I was drawn into it against my will...

There are surely bigger criminals in the world...

The mediator tried to console him with the thought that he was, after all, going home.

You have a home.

I don't even know if my home village is still standing.

Vatanescu was made to sign a bundle of documents, the contents of which were unknown to him and which no one took the trouble to explain to him. After a medical examination in the morning he would leave the country. He could choose either to travel by plane with an escort or in an old van, which he would have to drive back to his homeland himself. If he chose the latter he would receive a mileage allowance and daily expenses on which he would be able to live quite well in Romania for a couple of months.

The man and the woman shook hands with Vatanescu, nodding to him in a sympathetic way that said it wasn't them; it was the law and the system...

'Get your own country into shape and then we'll go there as tourists,' the woman said.

'I used to visit Bulgaria quite often during the Soviet era,' the man said. 'Good night then, Vatanescu. May I take one more photo…? My son wanted me to take one of you when he heard I was going to see you…'

My crazy useless journey…

'And if you could put your autograph on it, please. For Väpi.'

Now that I've talked, I have no value.

Life is a market.

Yegor was my only currency.

They've taken my future away.

I want the football boots.

Vatanescu heard the door of his room being locked for the night. He put the pills from the little cup in his mouth, took a sip of water and lay down. Within half an hour the medication worked, the pain in his stomach subsided, and reality dissolved in a grey mist.

Six hours later he was woken by the sound of chewing. Someone was eating Vatanescu's last democratic bowl of porridge. Vatanescu rubbed the sleep from his eyes and sat up on his bed. The sun filtered through a small window; there was coffee in a thermos flask and also, this morning, some slices of ham and cheese.

'*Morjens. Guten Morgen.* Good morning.'

My escort?

'No, it's Pahvi.'

Are you going to take me on the plane back to my homeland?

'Pahvi, Simo. Simo Pahvi. Let me shake your hand.'

Limp.

Sweaty.

Now he's pressing. Firmly. Will he look me in the eye?

Yes.

190

Something was moving in Simo Pahvi's inside pocket. He tut-tutted and opened his jacket. Then the rabbit leapt across his knee to the floor. For a moment it slipped on the linoleum, then bolted into Vatanescu's arms.

My friend.

Tired tears flowed from Vatanescu's eyes.

I thought…

…they told me that…

…you'd ended up as tiger food.

'They got it wrong, a misunderstanding,' Simo Pahvi said. 'They told me you'd been moved to the police cells, but you were here in the hospital all the time.'

We didn't die.

Vatanescu took the rabbit's face between his hands and looked into its eyes. It smacked its lips; it looked back at Vatanescu with the kind of trust that only a child can show towards its father. Or was it Vatanescu who looked at the rabbit that way? At any rate they were now together again and ready to meet the next incomprehensible sequence of events.

Simo Pahvi wiped his hands on his trousers and dislodged with a matchstick a grain of porridge that had got stuck between his teeth.

'Do you know who I am?' he asked in English.

No idea.

Simo Pahvi explained that he was the tribal chieftain of this land. The king. *Il capo di tutti capi*. He had a lot more power and authority than Yegor had ever had. Yegor's patch was tiny and it was rented. For four years Simo Pahvi owned every inch of the entire country, from lake to lake, from lowly housing estates all the way to the upmarket villas of Espoo's Westend.

I've already said all there is to be said about him.

'About Yegor Kugar? That fellow doesn't interest me one bit. He's the concern of Interpol now.'

My sister. There was talk of my sister.

'It's all right. I have a message from her.'

At Simo Pahvi's feet there was a Siwa supermarket plastic bag. It contained a video cassette. The hospital's recording systems were ten years behind the times, so it was not very hard to find a video cassette player. Pahvi studied it for a moment, unsure of which way to insert the cassette. The tape began to turn.

My sister.

Her hair is a different colour from when I left.

She's at an airport with signs in German.

My sister says that she is going as far away from Central and Eastern Europe as she can.

She thanks me.

But doesn't intend to join me, doesn't intend to come to a Nordic country. Has saved all the money she earned with her body, which isn't much, because seventy-five per cent went to the Organisation. But something, all the same. It was such a filthy job that she wants her money's worth now. She owes it to her body.

She's going to start a fitness centre.

Isn't going to start a family.

She's going to take out a bank savings bond.

Isn't going to succumb to drink or drugs.

Hopes that all is well with me. Hopes I will come and visit her. Hopes that I've managed, even though she hasn't been there to keep an eye on me.

Then the recording stopped; for a moment there was a hissing, and then some footage of an ice hockey match from several years back. Simo Pahvi turned the television off with the remote control. Vatanescu pressed the rabbit against his chest: swallowing all this was like eating nuts and bolts with pink iced doughnuts.

'Everything's all right there,' Pahvi said, opening

the carton of milk that was part of Vatanescu's breakfast. 'But what interests me is you.'

Me?

Who do you think I am? What's the matter with you all?

'You're not a criminal, Vatanescu.'

I never have been.

'Not in my eyes, and not in the eyes of the people.'

I've been a beggar. An investor. And a concrete layer.

'You, Vatanescu, are the highest form of existence.'

A magician?

'A celebrity.'

Vatanescu sat in the back seat of the Mercedes. The
car was new to him, but every Finn knew it as the
'Million Merc'. It had been bought new at a time when
support for the Ordinary Smallholders' Party stood
at more than fifteen per cent. The Merc had seen the
party's rise and fall and ruin; it had seen its revival and
present success, as had the driver, Esko Sirpale. The
'million' referred to the number of miles the car had
done. In the Merc they had planned election campaigns,
mourned the defeats of ice hockey teams and discussed
the growing pains of children. Simo Pahvi called it his
office.

The Million Merc suited Pahvi's style perfectly. It was
available to the general public; the average price of that
year's model was around a thousand euros, six hundred
and fifty if you haggled. To buy an Audi A8, in which
government ministers normally travelled, an ordinary
citizen would have to buy and sell companies, win the
lottery or rob a bank. A Million Merc, on the other hand,
was something you could save for out of your salary.

'The sills are rusted,' Simo Pahvi said to Vatanescu.

'Rust is a sign of life. It's the bosses who protect their sills. Cars like to be used.'

Inside the Merc there was a fusty odour of cigarette smoke, which covered any other smells. This was a vehicle in which Vatanescu felt at home; it was the kind in which he had made the journeys of his life whenever he had managed to travel by car. The Million Merc consumed as much oil as petrol, but that was not a problem for Simo Pahvi.

'This country was built with greasy hands,' he would say, as he had also said during the last prime minister's question time.

Pahvi rummaged in the Siwa bag for a suit for Vatanescu. The suit was deliberately ill-fitting and shabby.

'What football team do you support?'

The one that my son will play in.

Pahvi rummaged in the bag and hesitated between the scarves of Real Madrid, Helsinki Football Club and Steaua Bucuresti. He opted for the Finnish national team. There was a miniature scarf for the rabbit.

'Let's wait for the right moment. There's no point in putting it on and going there straight away.'

Where?

'Sorry for my bad English, but you don't seem to have an Oxford accent either.'

We understand each other.

In a language.

But I don't understand what I'm doing here.

'They can't deport you. It would start a national uprising. Good grief. The Church has promised to give you sanctuary.'

Me, Vatanescu?

'You've been discussed at the UN. The boot of the Merc is full of online petitions, soft toys and ladies' undergarments. A couple of men's too. All sent to you.'

Don't make fun of me. Please.

'You'll know when I'm making fun of you. Listen. Do you know what's most important in the politics of today, Vatanescu?'

The basic issues?

'The basic issues can be addressed by those who are interested in them. What interests me is influence. Influencing people. Persuading them. Having an effect. That's what politics is. Always has been.'

I don't know anything about politics.

I've never voted.

I don't know if I have the right to vote.

'Of course you bloody have. Everyone has. In a democracy every vote counts. Every vote is decisive. Do you know what my success is founded on?'

Vatanescu gazed at the corpulent, out-of-breath man who sat next to him. At first sight he didn't look like someone who had succeeded in the way that rappers and business moguls do.

'My success is founded on who I am.'

On corpulence and geniality?

'I know the masses; I can make them follow me. I'm a shepherd. People want to look down as well as up.'

What does that have to do with me?

What are you getting at?

'Human interest.'

Eh?

'The big issues need the face of the little man.'

You can't get much littler than me.

'But one shouldn't start being miserable, either. Look, I used to be the face of the little man. Now I'm taking a step forward and I'm no longer so little any more. No prime minister ever is, and a president even less. But there's a new face.'

I don't understand.
'It's yours, Vatanescu.'

Simo Pahvi asked Esko Sirpale to stop the car outside his favourite restaurant. This was the place where, at the most heated point of his election campaign, he had announced that immigrants had nothing to worry about. As long as they worked, like Ming Po.

After that, Ming's Palace had grown into a chain of restaurants that were in direct competition with the two biggest hamburger chains. One important reason was Simo Pahvi, and another that the new government brought in tax concessions for all the restaurants that had Karelian hotpot on their menus. From the Night Menu Pahvi ordered Number 18, the Finland Maiden. This pizza was blue and white, because of the cheese on it, and its principal ingredient was Finland Sausage.

'I'll take three. To go. Yes. And three milks.'

They ate in the back seat of the car.

'If you like, I'll tell you all about it while we eat.'

You don't need my permission.

'No, I don't! But, look. Perhaps you don't know how big you are.'

Five foot nine, a hundred and forty-seven pounds on the hospital scales.

'I mean figuratively. Listen, for several months now, Vatanescu, you've been bigger in the media... than... well, The Beatles. I'm not a young man any more. But you're still under forty. A man in his prime.'

'Keep it simple so he can understand it,' Esko Sirpale asked. 'Try to be clear.'

'Yes. Well. Vatanescu. I followed your journey all along, but I didn't realise your true worth until Jesus showed me.'

Christ?

'Mähönen. At first I wondered what to make of you… a global phenomenon and a ragamuffin. But then I got sort of hooked. Damn it, Vatanescu. You kept going straight ahead. With a straight back. A straight mind. Along a straight road. Didn't you?'

I was forced to.

I kept going so I wouldn't stop.

My journey had no other aim.

'Wherever you went, you did the job one hundred per cent, with style.'

I tried to manage.

I wanted the football boots.

'You never gave in to laziness or egoism. You saved the national park. You exposed corruption.'

I didn't set out to.

I'm sorry.

'You exposed the inflexible labour market and the ossified social security system. It really is true that here in the Last Outpost of the North we can't take the truth about ourselves unless it's expressed sort of stealthily, and by foreigners. Like the author Neil Hardwick, for example.'

A man I don't know.

Simo Pahvi ate his pizza starting from the edges, making a constant effort to attain the final climax, the centre where the Finland Sausage had fled its devourer. The cold milk flowed wonderfully down his gullet to his stomach.

'I'm going to bag you before my imitators do. Fortunately they need a PR agency for their plans. All I need is a pack of cigarettes.'

Simo Pahvi sprinkled his pizza with tabasco sauce and parmesan, and smiled a big, doggy smile.

'The socialists, the centre right, the Christians, the

tree-huggers. They always lag behind me.'

A broad face that looked as if it had been thrashed with a frying pan without suffering much damage apart from getting an even broader smile. Greasy hair, a pug nose, an ordinary carefree man who didn't try to stand out from the rest, but instead mixed in with the crowd.

'I had to give the whole of myself, because the others had nothing in them.'

I don't understand.

'Yes, you do! Behind me I drag a bunch of losers who can't even put the oars in the rowlocks!'

You're speaking figuratively?

'I'd like to. It's full. Stomach. There's food left. I stretch out my hand. The others eat out of it. I close my fist. They remain hungry. Do you understand that, too?'

You're speaking concretely?

'I'm speaking figuratively.'

Forgive me, Mr Simo, but what does this have to do with me?

'Vatanescu, I don't want my work to go to waste. You have to help me. I need you.'

You need a driver?

'Wait, I've got some notes about this.'

Simo Pahvi dug some cigarette packs out of his inside jacket pocket. They were covered with scribbles. Then he found the right one in the rear pocket of his trousers.

'Here. You come from elsewhere, like our former president, Martti Ahtisaari. You're soft, like our Orthodox clergyman MEP Father Mitro. And what about the rabbit?'

The rabbit was sitting on the pizza box eating a piece of sausage. Vatanescu put his hand on its back and scratched the hollow in the back of its neck.

'On your own you'd be a scary tramp. And on its own the rabbit would be a suspect bundle of germs.'

Now for the first time Simo Pahvi looked Vatanescu straight in the eye. Now for the first time Vatanescu began to understand what Pahvi was saying. The diamond-hard logic of his senseless talk.

'But together you're cuter than dear Father Mitro! Hell's bells, you're like Charlie Chaplin and the Kid. Even a grown man like me has a tear in his eye... and that's the great thing, Vatanescu. You can make people laugh and cry. You're a survivor and a man of resource. An everyman. You're not a trickster and you're not a coward. You're not a thief, even if you did borrow that Swede's car for a while.'

Esko Sirpale looked at Vatanescu in the rear mirror and nodded. This was clearly a plan that they shared, had devised together, were implementing together, like Simo Pahvi's election campaigns.

'If you know how to make people laugh and cry, the door of the safe is open to you,' Pahvi said. 'You've a landslide of votes at your disposal. The combination of laughter and tears makes people believe and hope. That's what life is about. Dreams, beliefs, hopes. Politics is the art of identifying those, and promising that they'll be fulfilled.'

Chapter Ten

In which Vatanescu grills ready-made honey-marinated chicken and forms a government

Miklos Vatanescu pedalled his three-speed bicycle back to the house from the mailbox. In the pile on the back carrier was a copy of the main national daily, the newspaper of the Ordinary People's Party, a mobile phone bill and a postcard sent from Lapland. The back of the card said:

> *Sicilian! Holy moly, you're a party leader!!!*
>
> *Congratulations!!! Let us know when the party wagon train rolls this way, the sauna is always hot for you, the rabbit and the gang! Bring the whole damn family, it's always nicer to drink with a big crowd!!! Even though I don't drink myself, or only a tiny drop! The wife sends you greetings! You'll never believe it, but I've taken up Zumba too, it has really transformed my evenings!!!*
>
> *P.S. I've had an idea for a statue!!! Outside the post office would be a great place for a statue to Arto Paasilinna, pioneer!!!*
>
> *All the best, Harri Pykström!!!*

Miklos took the mail up to the study on the first floor of the house, as he always did during the weeks when he stayed with his father. Right now the only person in the study was Uncle Simo, who invited him to sit in Vatanescu's chair. With brown eyes, a serious expression, gentle and calm, his father's son, Miklos Vatanescu sat down. In the Siwa bag Uncle Simo had a present for him.

The Siwa bag was a classic, in which Simo Pahvi carried work papers, contracts and several empty cigarette packs for taking notes on. The bag had also become the world's first pirated product, and the original, at twenty cents, cost less than a copy, at fifty-six euros. Simo rummaged in the bottom of the bag and produced a pair of football boots, which he placed on Vatanescu's desk.

'Do you know how to tie the laces?'

The boy shook his head. He smiled to himself. He had never owned shoes with laces. He was crying and shouting inwardly. His father had kept his word, Miklos now had football boots – and he also had his father back.

'Sometimes a foot grows too big, just as a political party can grow too big. The solution is to take the next size up.'

They tried the boots on him. They fitted perfectly.

'A party needs to have a growth margin,' Pahvi said, savouring his own words. 'Football boots don't. That could start an opening speech, couldn't it?'

Simo Pahvi tied the laces with double knots and told the boy to take a few running steps. He crushed the day's newspaper into a ball and threw it on the floor. Miklos flicked the ball in the air with the tip of one foot and onto the heel of the other, bouncing it several hundred times.

'Pick a jersey for yourself from the other bag.'

Miklos Vatanescu kicked the paper ball into the wastepaper basket and then sat down as children do, with his backside on the floor and his legs folded at his sides. He examined the different coloured jerseys and decided on Brazil Number 10. Pahvi thought this a far-sighted choice.

'A quality team, impartial. Multicoloured. Like Sweden, but further away. No historical trouble with Finland.'

Miklos found the jersey a bit tight against his skin at first, but when he saw himself in the mirror he forgot the tickling. Boots and a jersey, the happiest day of his life in Nurmijärvi.

'We'll keep the Finnish jersey for more important events,' Pahvi said. 'Let's go down and see how the chicken's cooking.'

Vatanescu's mother stood on a freshly cut lawn in a residential district of Nurmijärvi. She looked to the right and saw a row of identical houses with large gardens. She looked to the left and saw a row of identical houses with large gardens. She was outside because of her suspicions towards underfloor heating. It was like hellfire burning down below. Vatanescu had tried to explain to his mother that underfloor heating was not only energy-efficient but also a symbol of gentrification. Onwards we go, as a Finnish ice hockey player had said during Vatanescu's election campaign. The order of progress was: campfire, chimneyless hut, heat-storing fireplace, oil burner. And now the underfloor heating – combined with an air-source heat pump and a wood pellet burner, which Vatanescu had in his house. But his mother took some convincing, and she preferred to have earth and soil beneath her feet.

Vatanescu had solved his mother's housing problem by buying the cottage of Komar Tudos in his home village back in Romania. It had been dismantled timber by timber and taken to Nurmijärvi, to a shaded place in the north-west corner of the site, in the lee of three tall pine trees. And there Jeffersson and Õunap were already at work on the reassembly. Their hammers thudded, the numbered beams were snapped into place and those that had rotted most were replaced with new ones. In exchange Komar Tudos received half of a duplex built by the Finnish embassy and its trade mission. Komar moved into one side, and all the ghosts he knew moved into the other. The embassy threw a housewarming party at which his plum brandy and several whole pigs were consumed.

But not even this was good enough for Vatanescu's mother, as the house still had Komar's smell, and his restless ghosts.

Vatanescu's mother turned on her heel; the sun was dazzling her but it didn't warm the air in the way that it did back home. Here a person felt hot and cold at the same time.

On the steps of the house next door Mama Vatanescu saw her son's ex-wife Maria, who had no objections to underfloor heating at all. It had been the only efficient way to organise joint custody. Every second week Miklos Vatanescu stayed with his father in the main building or accompanied him on official visits. The rest of the time he spent with his mother in the guesthouse.

Maria greeted Mama Vatanescu, who growled in response, spat three times over her left shoulder, then over her right shoulder, then on the ground straight in front of her, with three snaps of the fingers of her right hand. The former mother-in-law was keeping her distance, so to speak, by putting a curse on her former daughter-in-law. Maria shrugged, put on her sunglasses and settled down in a hammock.

Mama Vatanescu turned round again and tried to detect which way the wind was blowing. Now she saw her son's house, a prefabricated dwelling with straight walls and an area of three hundred square metres. To Mama Vatanescu the house contained every modern convenience, but lacked character and history. However, each generation had its own aspirations and habits, which were always a source of bewilderment to the previous generation. Vatanescu was still her son, even though the world had moved on and changed. He still had the same curly hair, and in the mother's memory her son's tears and laughter were still preserved.

Leaning on her walking stick, she took a few short steps. Instead of being carved from knotted wood, as it would be back home, this stick bore the words 'Public Health Centre', and its tip could be fitted with a fine spike if required. She had also been offered a rollator and visits by Meals on Wheels, but turned them down and got out of the situation by resorting to her spitting ritual.

From round the corner in front of her Miklos arrived at a run. In his new jersey, dribbling a football in front of him with gleaming boots. The ball was like an extension of him, like a hand or a head; it always had been – he was 'a nifty lad', as they said in Vatanescu's family. His speciality involved placing the ball on the tip of his foot and performing a kind of somersault with a kinetic energy that sent the ball flying into the top corner at terrifying speed.

Miklos swung the ball between his grandmother's legs and then kicked it far away towards the shore. Simo Pahvi ran panting after, his shirtsleeves rolled up and his glasses misted over. He greeted Mama Vatanescu, who gave him an imperceptible nod. She found the warts on his neck suspicious, and she also thought that he looked too much like a walrus.

Mama Vatanescu climbed the steps to the veranda.

She asked her son what he was thinking, as his gloom could be felt halfway down the garden.

So much that's new. So many things to learn.

'No one can learn politics in a day.'

Not that. The instructions for this grill.

As housewarming presents Simo Pahvi had bought Vatanescu a large Calor gas barbecue grill, and a trampoline for Miklos.

'And what about everything else? My son, what about the rest of your life? Within you? In your heart?'

I'm not afraid of death any more.

I have life around me.

The magician hasn't got in touch with me. Perhaps she doesn't dare to?

Perhaps some time I'll call her again. One day I may have time for love. Pahvi thinks that politics come first.

Pahvi's housewarming gift package also contained a people carrier, an espresso machine and a hedge-trimmer. You had to know the habits, activities and aspirations of the electorate, he had said. You had to be able to speak their language. If the Ordinary People's Party wanted to reach upper-middle-class voters it had to understand what made the target group tick. That was why this evening Vatanescu was to grill a whole bucketful of ready-made honey-marinated chicken fillets.

Simo Pahvi climbed the steps to the veranda, his knees cracking. He took off his shirt and used it to wipe the back of his neck, the top of his head and the folds of his belly. Then he threw the shirt about his shoulders and approached Vatanescu.

'Problems, old chap? Feeling nervous about tonight?'

How do you turn on the gas?

'There are these little buttons. Look, you turn them like this...'

Then Simo Pahvi clicked the electric switch and held his hand over the grill tray for a moment. He spat on it and when the spittle began to boil he asked Vatanescu to open the packs of honey-marinated chicken.

'I can get them started.'

Vatanescu sat down beside his mother on the bench they had bought at the retail park along with the rest of the garden furniture. She took his hand in hers. They saw Miklos running about on the lawn, and the rabbit bouncing around at his feet. Boy and rabbit were passing the ball to each other, and now and then Miklos would shoot the ball towards a tree, a wall or his mother, who was resting in the hammock. The rabbit also had a hutch of its own on the edge of the forest, with a small carrot patch beside it.

The boy got them.

Football boots.

'This is how you do it,' Pahvi said, leaning over the grill. 'You don't want too many pieces next to one another, so they have room to be turned and the tray doesn't go cold. When the liquid comes to the surface you turn them. Actually it doesn't really matter how you turn pieces of chicken. A bit like political rivals. Some folk like their meat juicy, others like it dry. Same goes for women.'

Pahvi burst into his contagious, quaking laughter. His belly heaved and the veranda shook.

'I think we'll use cardboard plates so the ladies don't have to do the washing up. Choose cardboard – pahvi. Makes things easier.'

I've been successful, Mama. For once.

'You'll succeed at anything you put your mind to,' said Mama Vatanescu.

I've never been successful before.

'But after this you always will. Believe me. I believe in you. I brought you into the world.'

In Mother Russia, behind bogs and coniferous forests, permafrost and tumbledown cabins, was the penal colony where Yegor Kugar was shut up in a cell. Though he no longer had a typewriter, he stubbornly continued to tell his story with a pencil in the margins of a hymn-book or any piece of white paper that fell into his hands. Like Papillon, Yegor Kugar kept all his writings in an aluminium tube, carefully concealed in a place where the solarium did not shine.

But let Yegor Kugar tell it as he did in his book *Crooks Have Thick Skins*, which was a worldwide success.

'I was a political prisoner. I've talked to Khodorkovsky and I can tell you that I wasn't sent down for stabbing Vatanescu, but for giving the Tsar a bad name. The Tsar alone has the exclusive right to bring shame on Russia beyond the country's borders. So there I was, living in this syphilis and gonorrhoea centre up the Volga Bend. Nothing to write home about, really shitty. Each morning when I woke up I felt as though I was on the movie set of *One Day in the Life of Ivan Denisovich*. Not as the hero but as some average guy who had been picked up off the street and then left in a real labour camp, even though he was only supposed to do one day's filming.

'Then one day I got a letter.

'I don't get letters. I thought it must be from my mother – her money had run out or she needed an advance for her funeral.

'It wasn't Mama, it was Vatanescu.

'On the envelope there was some kind of fan photo or ministerial portrait. A rather kitschy photo, Vatanescu in the middle of a row of old guys in dark suits, with the rabbit. At first I thought it was some kind of cruel joke, turning the knife in the wound, but there really was a letter inside.

'Vatanescu wrote that he'd heard about my memoir project and was willing to find me a publisher for it, maybe Johnny Kniga or Bonniers, or straight into the US market.

'Whaaaat???!!!

'I admit that it fazed me a bit, but it was only the beginning. Vatanescu also said he had negotiated my release. He was such a big shot at the UN, at Greenpeace, Amnesty and in US foreign policy that saving me had been easy. The envelope contained instructions for the journey, and to start with a helicopter would take me to St Petersburg. There I would be given clean clothes, a clean passport and a train ticket.

'Whaaaaaaaaaaaaaaaaat???!!!'

And that was where Yegor Kugar went, back to Finland, to his first real job. He was given a tax deduction card, a taxi card and an identity card. He was destined for an important role in Vatanescu's first government.

'Of course I know the ways and customs of the Russian people, I speak the language and I know the social code. Like the man from Del Monte, I said yes! I accepted a post as an expert on East–West relations.'

The Million Merc took our hero, replete with ready-made honey-marinated chicken, to the city's stony centre. From now on his meals would be prepared by head chef Ming Po, who used the finest raw ingredients in the land to create an infinite combination of wonders and specialities from the seven great gastronomies of the world. When Ming made marinades, he used only the finest natural honey from Mäntsälä, soy sauce from Okinawa and maple syrup from Canada.

Esko Sirpale drove, and Jesus Mähönen sat beside him. Vatanescu, Miklos and Pahvi were in the back seat. In its search for a suitable lap the rabbit stopped on Miklos to be scratched.

Simo Pahvi wrote on the back of a cigarette pack with his carpenter's pencil, and smiled. His deeds were going to make populist history; this was going to alter the ship's course entirely; it would open the North–East passage. It wasn't a U-turn; it was a rebirth. Simo Pahvi would be remembered as the party leader who in place of narrow-mindedness, faction-alism and racist populism chose Vatanescu. Without losing anything of the original idea of the Ordinary People's Party, because Vatanescu was more ordinary than ordinary. The concept of positive populism had already spread from the small country of Finland to the world, and new sectors were being won over all the time. The Italian prime minister was interested in the new format, as were several parties in Belgium, France and the Netherlands. Faxes had arrived from both the Democrats and the Republicans in the United States. The party's support base had evolved from shell-suited chavs to consumers of soy sausage. With Vatanescu's help, Simo Pahvi had solved the problem of his own future and that of his party, while making all other parties unnecessary.

'Everything circulates,' Pahvi suggested as the title for that evening's television address.

Good circulates.

'Too flat,' Esko Sirpale said. 'We need something with a bit more edge.'

'We need one more word,' Jesus Mähönen said.

'Three words are enough. We just need to know what they are.'

'Ball,' said Miklos, who was looking out of the window at the football stadium. 'Have we got the ball with us?'

Good balls circulate.

'Hell's bells, Vatanescu, that's it!' Pahvi shouted, and wrote the phrase down on his cigarette pack. 'You'll be rolling that ball for the whole of your term in office! We've put a good ball into circulation. Let's play ball.'

A man is a ball.

Sometimes an empty one that needs to be pumped up again.

'Just so. Go on.'

A ball hits a wall, but bounces back again? A ball is always faster than a man?

'Exactly.'

What does it mean?

'Don't worry about that, Vatanescu. The public will fill in the gaps. And the ballot papers.'

Vatanescu nodded.

'Use your own life as an example. For everything. When they ask you for a solution to the beggar problem, tell them how it was for you.'

I wanted boots.

I also got a ball.

'And remember who you are.'

Vatanescu?

'You're the future. You're me. Remember your own value.'

What's that?

'Salary class: A1, competency class: A1, irreplaceability factor: A1.'

And the Million Merc rolled along Route 3 at forty miles an hour, for Esko Sirpale did not dare to drive the car any faster. But the slow speed was more imposing, more dignified and old-worldly than stepping on the gas would have been. Miklos Vatanescu scratched the rabbit under its chin, one eye on his football boots. Pahvi fished some neckties out of the Siwa bag and tried them on Vatanescu.

'Damn. That tie looks even worse on you than it does on me. We might as well just go around in tracksuits if we want to.'

Or snowsuits.

'I'm president. As of this evening you're prime minister. There was a Paasikivi Line and a Kekkonen Line. We lads are going to introduce the Tracksuit Line.'

Then Vatanescu's phone rang. He didn't know how to answer it, and handed it to his son. Miklos pressed the green button, listened for a moment and said to his father:

'It's someone called Sanna.'

*M*iklos was delivered at birth by his grandmother. Anneli, in her turn, was delivered by the midwife. Exactly nine months after our train journey.

I cut the umbilical cord.

A tiny little girl, the strangest and most peculiar creature in the world, full of demands and displeasure. And yet the most familiar and self-evident one, too.

She will have everything right from the start.

A birth is not a miracle. It will be the same until the end of time, until the last human being. The need for life, and also its meaning.

What was miraculous about the event of childbirth was how much attention both Sanna and the newborn child received, how important it was that everyone stayed alive. The attention that was given to making sure that the readings on the measuring devices were correct, that the blood tests were precise. That the baby's breathing was normal, that her appetite was growing, that her weight was increasing. That her life would continue. That another taxpayer was on the way.

Now I have a son and I have a daughter and they have all the vaccinations and toys and playsuits and football boots they need. I have a house, a mortgage and a family car. I have many more things, and stranger ones than I ever wished for. One can't wish for what one doesn't know exists.

The Last Chapter

In which a good rabbit circulates

This is not the end, for nothing in this life has an end except life itself. And even after decomposition it continues as a beautiful display of flowers or an intolerable growth of weeds, which people try to control with the help of lawnmowers and yellow gardening gloves. But poor humans can't control nature, because man is a part of it, and viewed from far enough away each one of us is a beautiful display of flowers or an intolerable growth of weeds.

In all this, after all this, what is the place of the animal, the rabbit? Does it have a place? Does it have a role and a value?

The rabbit did not enjoy the photo sessions, the official visits and the finely laid tables. The rabbit hopped away down the long tables to hide in a cupboard when the presidents, monarchs and dictators expressed a desire to stroke and pat it. When the animal liberationists wanted to liberate it, it fled into the darkest corner. Its pulse raced, it slept badly, it put its ears back and stopped eating. When an attempt was made to take sentimental pictures of the rabbit and Anneli Vatanescu-Pommakka for the lead story in a women's magazine, the rabbit disappeared for several days and was eventually found in an air-conditioning duct, badly dehydrated.

Above all, the rabbit did not like Vatanescu's new duties as a father, a politician and a member of civilisation. In the hierarchy of the needs of someone living under normal conditions, a rabbit becomes a domestic pet, a cherished one to be sure, but no longer a brother, a comrade or a travelling companion.

'An animal can't live the life of a human being,' Vatanescu's mother said. 'It doesn't care for luxury any more than I do.'

'You can't get rid of the rabbit,' Simo Pahvi said for his part. 'It secured you half your votes. We can't afford to get rid of it.'

It won't survive one more foreign trip.

'We'll get some doubles. Who'll notice the difference?'

I wouldn't exchange my children if they were frightened of the new.

But the worst was still to come. At her half-yearly medical examination it was discovered that Anneli Vatanescu-Pommakka was allergic to milk and animals. It was at once clear what caused her spots, shortness of breath and red eyes. She had been born in a world where hair was something dirty and superfluous, unlike her big brother Miklos, whose body was used to animal fur, human leavings and the significant damage caused to floors by dampness.

'We can't keep it,' said Sanna. 'You know that. We just can't.'

It's true.

It's impossible.

For seven days and nights Vatanescu said not a word.

'Talk to me,' Sanna demanded. 'Please don't bottle it all up, dear. How can you have become… such a… so… Finnish?'

I can't keep bustling around all the time; the world goes on nevertheless.

I don't like talking.

I like pottering in the garage. I have a beer, maybe even another beer, sometimes Pykström calls me when he's doing the same. I have a few tipples.

And even though I rack my brains about the rabbit, I can't come up with a solution.

The rabbit will just have to take what it has to take. That's what I did.

Soon the rabbit also began to show symptoms. It sneezed, its eyes became red and it didn't like being outside any more. Vatanescu took it to the vet, who quickly produced a diagnosis. The animal was allergic to infant humans. Its respiratory organs would not tolerate air conditioning, let alone transcontinental flights. Moreover, it clearly didn't get enough sleep and exercise.

'It's a psychosomatic syndrome,' said the vet. 'If it were human I'd give it a course of Cipramil. But for an animal I won't prescribe anything. I'd encourage you to find a natural solution.'

Vatanescu returned from the vet's more perplexed than ever, without a solution, at a dead end.

I've found a home and a family. Each night I get into my own bed, in my own home, because a person needs a home to leave and come back to. One can't be on a journey all the time; a journey is something that's temporary.

Money from one's job, food from the supermarket, children from the kindergarten, berries from the bushes, fish from the lake, insurance from the insurance company, a loan from the bank, the wife from her dancing, treatment from the hospital.

Then home.

To one's family circle.

Until one has it one doesn't realise what it's worth.

Vatanescu stroked the rabbit's side.

He noticed that his hand was trembling, his chin unsteady.

We've shared our journey.
But my house can't be your house.

Sirpale stopped the car in front of the mailbox, where a letter for Vatanescu was waiting.

Dear Prime Minister,

You won't remember, but I'm Pentti Körmylä. We dined at the same table on the Stockholm ferry. You looked at us and we wondered who that dark chap sitting there was. It all came back to me when you started appearing on TV and radio. I noticed how you weighed your words. That's a good thing. But the fact that you are also able to choose those few words correctly is more rare. My wife and I read in a ladies' magazine that you originally came here in order to buy a pair of football boots for your son. We have a pair for which we have no use.

Ulla Körmylä here, good evening, Mr Prime Minister. It feels a bit embarrassing to write to you about a thing like this, but Pentti and I decided that it was now or never. The fact is that back in 1956 we were due to have a child. We even thought of a name for it. Violet.

Martti.

Pentti is talking nonsense. The name was Violet. But in the end we never had the child, and I don't want to bore you with the details. Although you look after the welfare of people in general, one can't expect you to be interested in the bygone troubles of a couple who are as old as Methuselah. Yet the details are painful, and for me they awaken many memories I would prefer to forget forever. Because in life it's important to look forward to tomorrow. Pentti doesn't believe in divine dispensation. But I have

*always let him keep his opinions, even the wrong ones,
because someone much wiser than us has decided that we
are to live our lives together. Not that anyone has ever
asked Pentti and me for our opinion. But I digress. If you
would like them, the football boots are yours. Pentti wants
to write a few words again.*

*Real leather. Just like the ones that the legendary Aulis
Rytkönen wore that year.*

*You can come and fetch the boots from us at our address:
597 Forest Close. I would put them in the post, but we
have no post office in our village any more. Perhaps you
could see if it's possible for them to give us our post office
back, and also our village shop. You will recognise our
garden by its tall oak tree. It was planted in 1956, that
tree, and its name is Violet.*

Martti.

*You will also be able to recognise our house because the
lights will be on. The other houses are empty. If I remember
rightly the Hillanens were the last to move, that summer
when there were an awful lot of mosquitoes.*

*Greetings,
  Ulla and Pentti*

*P.S. The key will be under the flowerpot if we're not at
home. Make yourself coffee, there is always some in the
box marked Co-op. But why would we leave our own
house? My knees can't manage the hills going down, and
Ulla's can't manage them going up.*

Vatanescu had that letter with him when one day in August he opened the Lahti agricultural show. He ate grilled sausages with his son, drank coffee in a disposable cup and listened to the voice of the people. There was a lot of it, that voice, and it varied both in volume and in content. Vatanescu had learned how to hold his cup lightly so that his fingers didn't get scalded, and the deposits of mustard and ketchup on the hotdog wrapping paper no longer made him shudder. Simo Pahvi had taught him the importance of mastering gestures, posture and a convincing laugh. Even though pretending, he had to give an impression of deep and real sincerity. Most important of all, he had had to master the language, so that there would no longer be any distance between him and the natives. And after several months of language courses both intensive and hypnotic, he now understood and spoke Finnish surprisingly well.

He threw away the disposable cup, sucked the inside of the sausage and ate the skin as well. He shook hands with various interest groups and let them take photographs of him and Miklos. At the exhibitors' request, they went to look at a Karelian herd bull and a drivable lawnmower from Minnesota, and the local football club presented Miklos with a jersey that had the number ten and the name Litmanen on the back. Another cup of coffee with a talkative local councillor, and then father and son returned to the back seat of the Million Merc.

Anneli Vatanescu-Pommakka was placed in her safety seat in the front of the car, and the rabbit crouched in a corner in the back.

'Shall I take the long way home?' Esko Sirpale asked.

Yes. The gravel and the potholes remind me of my childhood.

'Perfect. But I'll have a little music. These songs remind me of my youth.'

Vatanescu had tried to understand the words, tried to catch the mood, but the sound of this land was so melancholy that it did not open up to him. Except for a few foreign songs like 'Genghis Khan' whose singer, Frederik, had performed at Vatanescu's victory concert on Helsinki's Tapulikaupunki Square. And as Frederik now sang 'Ramaya', Vatanescu stretched forward to the front seat to tickle his daughter under her chin. Then he tickled the rabbit's neck. Both daughter and rabbit sneezed. Esko Sirpale wound down the front windows, and Vatanescu the rear ones.

Vatanescu looked at the countryside with its fields, its wooden churches, its cowsheds, cemeteries, shopping centres with towers that reached to the sky, its service stations, moped riders, girls with bare midriffs, boys in baggy trousers, all the things that had been totally strange to him but now were forever familiar.

They arrived at yet another village, no different from the rest except for its name and the height of its church tower. Sirpale let the car roll past the cemetery; a squirrel climbed up the trunk of a spruce tree, jumping from branch to branch.

'If you want to see *Sports Roundup* at home we'd better go back by the motorway.'

We have a more important matter to attend to now, one that affects a whole life.

Miklos can enter the address on the satnav.

597 Forest Close.

The paint was peeling, but the house stood at the top of the hill, straight as an oak. It had been built with modest means, as well as possible, with self-felled timber, on gravelly soil. Reason and moderation, dream and reality. There was a small potato patch, with currant bushes at regular intervals. At the bottom of the garden was a woodshed, with two neat stacks of firewood. There was a garden hose, a lawnmower, an axe, a saw and a chainsaw.

'What are we going to do here?' Miklos asked his father.

The owner knows the value of things. It doesn't depend on their age.

It's their usefulness and their sentimental value.

No one wants to lose what's valuable.

Whoever built that shed is afraid of losing it. So he protects it and treasures it.

On the porch sat an elderly couple with grey hair and wrinkled faces, the man in a short-sleeved shirt and the woman in a summer dress. The woman's head rested on her husband's shoulder and they loved each other with the same tenderness they had shown on the Stockholm ferry. The depth of their feelings was confirmed by how the sight moved Vatanescu and startled Miklos. When Pentti saw the guests, he got up with difficulty and extended his hand.

'We've been waiting for you every day.' he said. 'Good boots for a good boy.'

'Eh?' said Miklos.

Ulla fetched her better, gold-rimmed cups from the dresser and served coffee for Vatanescu. For Miklos there was a mug, fruit squash and a parcel wrapped in brown paper and tied with string. Vatanescu looked at the couple and then at his son, who was silently eating a large hunk of coffee bread. He followed it with a second

Tuomas Kyrö

hunk, and a third. He examined the football boots, he breathed in the smell of real leather, felt the tips of the toes. The boots were heavy, came from a different time, creaked. Never in a million years would he wear them; they would ruin his reputation and his athletic ability, but he had been brought up by his grandmother and he knew the right words to use so as not to offend the old couple.

'They're really valuable,' he said. 'They'd probably fetch hundreds of euros on an auction website.'

Ulla took Pentti's hand and stroked it, then passed her hand over his rough cheek for a moment.

'And the rabbit, we really adore it,' Ulla said. 'Do you have it with you?'

While Ulla inquired after the rabbit, Esko Sirpale removed the safety seat from the front of the car, got out and brought a tearful Anneli to Vatanescu. The rabbit also tried to escape through the open door, but it was shut in front of its nose. Long gone were the days of its freedom, the open road, its indispensable role in surprising turns of events. Now it had become either an extension of Vatanescu or a soft toy enclosed by four walls, without having sought either role. It bounced from the gearstick onto the back seat and then up to the rear window ledge.

From there it watched the humans recede, and heard the unpleasant sound of crying grow fainter. If it could, the rabbit would have covered its ears with its paws in order not to hear that noise. Human offspring were a strange force of nature engaged either in defecating, vomiting or smiling, the last of which the rabbit knew to be only a sign of wind anyway, and yet in those who looked after them they awoke enormous feelings of love and a desire to protect. These feelings in turn became

221

houses, cars, insurance policies, summer cottages, holiday villages, playgrounds, educational institutions and amusement parks. The rabbit did not understand why human infants cried, for animals didn't cry; they learned to cope as soon as they were able to walk. They couldn't afford to cry, as there was always a fox or a hunter or a hawk about somewhere.

But this wasn't really crying. Rather, it was a request and a demand.

Anneli was saying she was hungry, and she shook her little fist in the air to emphasise the fact.

Ulla got up from her chair to look at the child, and quietly sang to her. The grandfather clock ticked from the wall. The refrigerator gave a rattling snore now and then – as did Pentti – and Ulla touched the tip of Anneli Vatanescu-Pommakka's nose, whereupon the little girl's crying stopped for a moment. Vatanescu took the child out of the baby seat and calmed her, then fished a bottle with a teat and a carton of baby milk out of his brief-case. With the ease of an expert he unscrewed the teat, opened the carton with his teeth and poured the correct amount into the bottle.

*D*rink your milk, little one who was conceived on the train. They would have made good parents. They have a house that was made for it, a solid post-war veterans' house. Flexible interiors, an unused room upstairs.

A wide, well-tended stretch of forest, with clear bounda-ries. A reasonable number of wild nocturnal carnivores.

There's a carrot patch and a potato patch.

All they need now is a child, who would be happy living there.

They will still make good parents.
Drink your milk, little one.

The window on the driver's side was partly open. The rabbit, forgotten and thirsty, wriggled its way out and wondered if it should leap away across the fields into the wilds or out onto the road to dash about in desperation this way and that, as others of its species had done as their last deed. The rabbit saw Vatanescu inside the house with the baby on his knee. The rabbit saw Miklos helping himself to a fourth hunk of coffee bread. The rabbit studied Pentti and Ulla, Ulla and Pentti, and through the porch flowed something powerful, something that only an animal could sense without a word being exchanged. The rabbit looked at the little boy who had ignited into being within the old man when Miklos arrived, and the surge of protective care in the old woman when the little baby was also present. The rabbit quietly hopped towards the gently crumbling concrete steps of the veterans' house, put its paws on the first step, then on the second, pushed its small head through the doorway and slipped inside. It bounded over the rag rug, traversed the tip of Esko Sirpale's foot and jumped up on the bench. From there it leapt onto the table, circumnavigating a pack of butter, a carton of whole milk and a tin of anchovies, and arrived in front of Ulla and Pentti. The rabbit threw itself onto Ulla's lap. The rabbit turned its gaze on Pentti, the rabbit turned its gaze on Ulla, the rabbit smelled the smells of this home, the smell of flannel, of sweat, of resin, of tar, of yeast bread and pine soap. The rabbit made itself into a warm, homely bundle. The rabbit instantly made itself irreplaceable, Ulla and Pentti's very own Violet or Martti.

Good rabbits circulate, we might think, as Ulla and Pentti make a nest for the rabbit in a cardboard box. Lousy Mercs roll, we might think, as Esko Sirpale steers the car along the forest road towards the highways, towards the rest of the life that is beginning on this day.

Esko Sirpale puts a cassette in the car stereo; it is one of Tapio Rautavaara's best songs, and even Vatanescu knows the tune and the words, because this song about the Sandman is the one that is certain to make Anneli Vatanescu-Pommakka fall asleep, and Vatanescu himself, and all of his numerous family, and the whole of Finland too, because it's a good song to fall asleep to.

> *...and he has a car that is blue*
> *and that car hums along unseen*
> *whirs and whirs as it carries you*
> *to the blue land of the dream...*